THE WARRIOR

THE WARRIOR

Wade Everett

GUNSMOKE

First published in the UK by Collins

This hardback edition 2011
by AudioGO Ltd
by arrangement with
Golden West Literary Agency

ISBN 978 1 445 85681 0

British Library Cataloguing in Publication Data available.

Printed and bound in Great Britain by
MPG Books Group Limited

Chapter One

Fort Riley, Kansas, sweltered under a freakish May heat wave. The sergeant major, who had been stationed there since '75, could not recall anything like it, and his duty at the post spanned nearly twenty years. For three days now not a breath of air had stirred, and the flag was a limp, colorful rag against the weathered flagpole. Smoke from the recruit mess rose in a sluggish smudge against a cloudless sky.

Flies swarmed and bit savagely, as though they were expecting a change in the weather, but none was promised, at least not by any of the usual signs. Duty was performed reluctantly, and recruits drilled and sweated. Dust rose and settled on them without moving laterally an inch, and tempers grew short.

In front of headquarters a row of generals' flags sagged from their diagonal poles, and the guards clung to the shade of the porch and knew that it was cooler there, although it didn't feel like it.

Inside, the general retirement board met; this was their third day, and there was little hope of an early adjournment. They had come to this post by train—two from Washington and one from the Presidio of San Francisco, one from Texas and another from Ohio, and their duty, their obligation, was common knowledge to the newest recruit on the post. They met every three years to weed and screen and pare away and cut down on military expenditures by surveying out military posts that no longer fitted into the overall changing picture. This was a ticklish business, for posts were closed and others were reactivated, and it just wouldn't do to be careless and bring down the wrath of some powerful politician, especially when you were going to ask him to approve of next year's budget.

The decision of the retirement board was not binding with the Secretary of War, but no one could recall a time when its decision had not been upheld and perhaps even questioned.

So they spent three days in the sweltering heat, smoking cigars and drinking coffee, and when the arguments got tight, they drank a little whiskey. But in that time they had agreed on a list of posts that would be closed, and others, now closed, that would be reopened.

It meant a great shuffling of troops and equipment and changes of assignment for a lot of officers, but it gave the military something to do. This was 1892, and the battle of Wounded Knee was nearly two years old, history now, and there were no more Indians to fight, and the army was feeling a little lost and bewildered by it all.

The day of the drawn saber and the charge had passed into memory, and the retirement board had to cut a big slice out of the officer corps. They had reached the conclusion that they had to retire one hundred and forty officers who had fought Indians for thirty years.

This had to be; you cut an army down from the

top, and with each officer nearly a hundred enlisted men would go beause many would not reenlist and recruitment would slow down. In a year the army would be trimmed down, and none of it would cause a ripple in the national economy.

Gen. Harvard Calhoun was the chairman of the board—a plump moose of a man with a huge head and a florid face that seemed always on the verge of rage. He was a man inclined to be bizarre in his dress and personal habits. With a little imagination a man not accustomed to the military could deduce that Calhoun was some kind of soldier, for his trousers were blue and had the familiar cavalry stripe running down the outside seam. His belt and buttons, although not regulation, bore insignia, so that one put him down as being on our side. He wore white ruffled shirts and dark string ties, and this marked him among the officer corps as a man who was inclined to take liberties for himself and to allow none to others.

General Calhoun wore two stars on his flag and saddle blanket, which put him up high enough so that very few could argue with him and none contradict him, but for the purposes of board efficiency all the general officers convened were considered equal.

This was not lighthearted duty, and non of them considered it so, for they were the counterpart of the promotion board, which sat and studied records and files and either raised the thumb or turned it down on a man's career. To be passed over by this board three times ended forever an officer's hope for promotion, for it put a stain on him, a reasonless stigma that just never came off.

There was no connection between the promotion board and the retirement board, except the records, and every member of the retirement board had studied the records and prepared his own lists. The records had been shipped on ahead, under guard, and were available to the staff of clerks who worked in an adjoining office.

Every man who had been twice passed over by the promotion board was on the list, and his file was there to be studied. The ones who had long ago been three times passed over were on separate lists. General Spencer, the youngest member of the board and most impatient, made a motion that these men be retired without further discussion.

Spencer was in his mid-forties, just getting gray at the temples. He was a singularly handsome man with a classic profile and commanding brown eyes. A bachelor, Spencer had been linked romantically from time to time with several socially prominent names, but no hint of indiscretion had ever touched him. He had a reputation for relentlessness, and he was entirely ruthless when it came to his own advancement and career.

"Any man who has spent twenty years in grade is too poor an officer to remain in the service," Spencer said. "Do I hear a second on my motion?"

General Calhoun kindled a fresh cigar and poured a cup of coffee. "Adam, this is your first retirement board. You may learn a thing or two." He looked at the others. "Would you care to discuss it?"

General Kicheloe, a rail of a man with dark, penetrating eyes, said, "I would like to exclude Capt. John Early from the list."

"Who," Spencer asked, "is John Early?"

Calhoun said, "Captain Early graduated sixth in the class of '66. He served with Crook in Arizona and lost his left eye. I sat on the retirement board for the first time in '71, and I wanted to retire him. He fought it and won. The next promotion board made him a first lieutenant. Besides, the Sioux campaigns were getting under way, and the army needed him. In '77 he lost his right arm just above the elbow in an engagement with the Sioux. Again he was up before the board, but the promotion board made him a captain, and we passed him over because Crook was having trouble in Arizona and requested him. Then he served with Miles in the '80s and was so severely wounded in the right leg that he was hospitalized for nearly a year. Even now he walks with a decided limp." He let his glance go around the table. "The promotion board passed him over, and we got him again. Do you remember that, Kicheloe? It was your first board."

"Mine, too," General Simmons said evenly. He was a small man, very slight of build, but he had a firm, resolute face and the eyes of a man who just won't be crossed.

"In the final days of the Sioux campaigns John Early distinguished himself on three separate occasions," Calhoun said. "The man won a Medal of Honor, one of the three given out in thirty years of Indian fighting."

"General," Spencer said, "I think we have to be firm about this. I see he's been passed over twice for promotion, and he's entitled to retirement, a life of ease."

"Ease? He wouldn't know what you're talking about," Kicheloe said. "I want him off the list." He leaned his elbows on the table and looked around. "I agree with Harvard; John Early is retained."

"If you had a command, sir," Spencer said, "would you accept him as a line officer?" He held up his hand. "I withdraw the question. Gentlemen, the complexion of the military has changed, and we've got to face it. Instead of fighting Indians, we now have to protect them on reservations. Now we've already agreed to reactivate a number of posts and transfer troops there for the sole purpose of policing the reservations. Naturally the post commanders will work hand in glove with the Bureau of Indian Affairs. Peace—that's what they'll be keeping. A singular role for singular men. Don't you agree?"

Calhoun's eyebrows arched, and General Buell, who said very little, let his attention sharpen. "Make your point," he suggested.

"Very well, sir, and bluntly. I propose that we go through this list most carefully, gentlemen, and look for men like Early, men who should have been out long ago, but who have been retained for one immediate military reason or another." He smiled. "I would never presume to suggest that any of you have acted out of sentimentality or loyalty to men like Early. However, we may find these men most useful in the coming years of confusion and uncertainty. To make it plainer, none of us know how to regulate Indian affairs. It's a new role, and tragic mistakes are bound to be made." He spread his hands. "I cannot see any merit in throwing the élite of the officer corps into the grinding jaws of public opinion. Are we to leave them with damning blots on their records? Why not select men we can afford to lose and let them make the mistakes? They can be observed, their reports studied, and in five or ten years good men can go in there and do the job right."

"That's the most damnable thing I've ever heard," Simmons said, "and I've heard some pretty rotten things. I don't say that you're not right, Spencer, but it still doesn't improve the flavor of it."

Kicheloe cleared his throat and prepared a cigar for the match; it was a ritual—licking the tobacco and smoothing it. "I think we should consider Spencer's argument to the extent that we draw on the retirement list to staff the officer force on the posts we have reactivated for this—Indian police duty. As you have pointed out, there are men we still might want to retain."

Spencer smiled. "Plainly put, gentlemen, we should fill these posts with men we may feel are not an asset to the service. And since Captain Early's name came up, I suggest that we give him command of Camp Sheridan near the Pine Ridge Agency. After all, he's a veteran of Wounded Knee, and the terrain will be familiar to him, and no doubt he'll know many of the Indians on the reservation." He looked around the table. "I'm open to argument, gentlemen." There was none; he hadn't expected any. "I have a man on the list, Lt. Joseph Deacon, as Early's adjutant. Sixteen years ago he seduced his commanding officer's wife. She promptly bought a ticket East and vanished, and her husband accused Deacon in front of the entire command, then blew his brains out in the confines of his quarters. I was the presiding officer at the board of inquiry, and I still feel it was a pity I couldn't have had Deacon cashiered."

Simmons frowned. "But you made sure he was never promoted. Three times passed over."

"It was the least I could do," Spencer said self-righteously. "Lover Joe. What post commander wanted him after that?"

Harvard Calhoun said, "Spencer, someday you will be the ranking general in the army, and I hope I never live to see it. I like my army with some life, some humanity in it. God, man, we're all frail!"

"I hope I am not," Spencer said. "Shall we go on?"

General Kicheloe sighed and said, "Here's a name: Second Lt. Harry Kitchen. Twenty-two years old?" He looked up. "What the hell is a man that age doing on this list?"

Gen. Nathan Buell said, "He married an Indian woman. She died. Left a son." He looked up from his fingernail paring. "You know how it is, Walter. That type of thing isn't done. I've got him in Texas now. Things are none too good down there, with Negro and Mexican feeling rather high. Being an Indian in Texas is even worse."

"He's cavalry," Kicheloe said, consulting the list. "Give him to Early. Maybe it won't matter so much there. That's a hard thing to say, but I didn't make the damned rules. I knew a captain once who married an enlisted man's daughter. He wiped out his career with those vows."

"There is one thing I enjoy about the military service," General Simmons said. "And that is that all decisions are made dispassionately and based on pure, mathematical logic. No emotions, no dogma to clutter the mind. Right, gentlemen?"

He looked at each of them, then laughed and got up and poured a drink of whiskey for himself. "All right, I've got one. First Lt. Murray Butler. Passed over by the promotion board for the third time fourteen years ago."

Spencer swept his finger down the list. "Fifty-four years old? Really, gentlemen, why wasn't this man retired years ago?" He looked around, waiting for his answer.

Kicheloe said, "Butler was in my graduating class nearly thirty-five years ago. God knows how he made it; he was dead last. He had eye trouble at the time. Wore glasses and tried to keep the super from knowing it and kicking him out. Ended up in artillery, and in '64 he lost his glasses, and because he couldn't see any distance, half a company got caught in the grapeshot from their own guns." He sighed and shook his head. "I haven't answered your question, have I, Spencer?"

"No, sir, you haven't."

"Well, what was the army going to do with Murray Butler? They stuck him in records and he spent eleven years there. Became quite a scholar without anyone ever knowing it. Sat in his office with his thick glasses, noticed by no one, writing papers and studying."

"Writing what?" Spencer asked.

"Dictionaries," Kicheloe said. "Dictionaries of the Choctaw language, the Sioux languages and dialects, the Apache language." He laughed. "Before we knew it, Murray Butler was the foremost expert on Indian languages and culture. He spent half his time on lecture tours. That's why he's been passed over on retirement. We need him. He's made great contributions and will likely go on making them."

Spencer consulted the list again. "He's in Arizona now."

"He goes and comes where he pleases," Kicheloe said. "Right now he's on his fourth year at the San Carlos reservation, working with the Apaches, teaching them how to raise grain and cattle." He looked at each of them. "Gentlemen, I'd like to ask Lieutenant Butler if he'd like to go to Camp Sheridan with Captain Early."

"I think that's an excellent idea," Simmons agreed, and all but Spencer nodded.

"Just a moment," Spencer said. "*Ask* him? A lieutenant?"

Kicheloe chuckled. "Adam, I know you deserve the experience; it's very good for general officers because it reminds them that they are not all-powerful and God-like. Lieutenant Butler doesn't give a good damn about the army for the simple reason that the army has never cared about him. If we retired him, any college would pay him three times his salary to teach, and he knows it. A colonel, I recall, was the last officer to give Murray Butler an order, and I think the colonel still regrets it. So I think we'll *ask* Lieutenant Butler. Agreed?"

They all nodded, even Adam Spencer, who felt that giving in weakened him a little. "No man is immune from a court-martial," he said stiffly.

"You're talking nonsense, Spencer," Simmons

said rather sharply. "Let's get on with it. The day's wearing out, and there's no relief from this damned heat."

As soon as his orders arrived, Capt. John Early packed his three suitcases and took the first west-bound train to Fort Robinson. When he reached there, he presented his orders to the adjutant, who saw that he had temporary quarters. Military manners dictated that he present his card to the commanding officer, but it was afternoon of the next day before he was summoned to headquarters, a delay Early had expected, for he was of little importance and deserved no special treatment.

Colonel Barlow commanded—a stern man who believed that an iron hand was the best weapon ever devised by man. He answered Early's left-handed salute as though he personally blamed Early for getting the wrong arm shot off. "Sit down, Captain. I have a lengthy dispatch from General Simmons. You're to use my post as a staging area. I trust you'll not clutter it unduly or delay your departure."

"My intention is to assemble a company as quickly as possible and leave. The others can follow." Early balanced his kepi on his knee. "During my stay here I imagine that my duties will so occupy me that I'll have little time for social activity, which should relieve the colonel's mind."

Barlow had a sharp face and the habit of puckering his expression to make it sharper. "I'm not sure I know what you mean, Early. And if I do know, I don't like it."

"That's quite understandable, sir," Early said.

"George, I know that you're under no obligation to me, but I would like at least one good sergeant."

"Every enlisted man I transfer to your command will be a qualified soldier," Barlow cut in. "And don't you think otherwise."

"That was very carefully put," Early said. "And I imagine every one of them will have had guardhouse time."

"Most soldiers do." He leaned forward. "John, did you ever know a post commander who had enough men? Or enough of anything? Well, I don't like it when an order comes down to me and strips me of a company. I like it even less when another officer is given the authority to select or reject what's been of-fered."

John Early smiled. "Sir, if I didn't have that right, I'd end up with every malcontent and guardhouse lawyer in the regiment. Will there be anything else?"

"No, that's all," Barlow said and answered Early's salute.

When he stepped out onto the porch, Early found that he knew no irritation; he rather thought of him-self as a bit lucky. Barlow could have had his back really humped and made it tough; he had enough reasons that went back twenty years, and he was the kind of man that would remember.

A soldier walking across the parade ground on the far side caught Early's eye; the man looked like a large ball propelled by short, stumpy legs. "Sergeant Deeter!" Early snapped.

The ball stopped, did a right face, found Early on the porch, then broke post regulations and cut right across the grass. He walked rapidly; it was almost a run. Then he saluted and shook Early's hand. "Captain, I see it and I don't believe it!"

"How have you been, Deeter?"

"Oh, I stay sober, sir." He pointed to a diamond above his hooks. "Top soldier, sir. Bet you thought I'd never make it."

"There were times when I wondered," Early said. "I'm assigned to Quarters G. Could you tell me—"

"I'll walk you there, sir. Is that your luggage?" He grabbed it and picked it up as though it weighed nothing. He fell into step with Early and they skirted the parade ground, walking around to a row of bachelor officers' quarters.

The room assigned to Early was usually given to lieutenants. He suspected that this was a deliberate slight, but he didn't care. Sergeant Deeter put the bags down and said, "I'll fetch you some fresh water, sir."

"That's a private's job."

Deeter grinned. "I served under you as a private, so this is for old times' sake."

He went out and a moment later came back with two large wooden buckets. Early had his shirt off and was preparing to shave. He stropped his razor by holding the strap between his knees; he had learned to do things without effort, things most men used two hands for.

"Sit down, Sergeant," Early said. "Unless you have duty."

"No, I was only going to the sutler's for a beer," Deeter said.

Early faced the mirror and lathered his face. He was forty-eight years old, and many of them had been hard years, years that had taken things out of him that had never been put back in. He was quite tall. His face was rather long, and his nose was all gristle and ridge, and a full moustache nearly hid his mouth. Lines like cracks in dried clay ran from the corners of his eyes; a patch covered the left eye, the band going around the back of his head. The right sleeve of his undershirt had been cut off, revealing the puckered stump; he had considerable use of that and held the towel under it while he shaved.

"I suppose you've heard that Camp Sheridan is being reactivated," Early said.

"The rumor's been going around." Deeter smiled. "I've already put in for a transfer, sir. I did that three days ago when I found out you'd be post commander."

Early turned his head and looked at the fat man. "Deeter, I kicked you out of my company on three separate occasions. Don't you ever learn?"

"I'm a top soldier now, Captain. That's as far as I'll ever go. So I figure I can pick and choose. And if I wasn't, I'd still want to transfer."

"You're a damned fool," Early told him and finished his shave. "You know good and well that a man in my company never stood a chance of being promoted."

"I know. That's why you kicked me out, so I could make sergeant, and then first. Captain, meaning no disrespect, but what makes officers so stupid?" He was walking on a thin crust and knew it, but it was a chance he was willing to take. "I soldiered with you, sir, when you had two eyes and two arms and could take the measure of any man. And I've sol-

diered with you since, sir, and damn it, I see no difference—"

"Don't let it bother you," Early said and slipped
into his shirt. "Deeter, I want to stay in the army. It's
that simple. But I'll never go to sixty-five, and I know
it. Every time a retirement board meets I get sick to
my stomach, but somehow they've passed me over.
Now I've been given command of a post. It won't be
much, and the duty will be the short end of the
stick, but it'll be duty, Deeter. It'll be service, and
that's enough for me."

"Me, too, sir. Will you accept my transfer?"

"Yes," Early said. "And you honor me, Sergeant."

"I got a couple of duty sergeants who'll listen to
some moral persuasion, sir."

"Now I don't want anyone reporting to me with a
black eye," Early said. "Strictly volunteers, Sergeant."

"That's what I've had in mind, sir. I did say moral
persuasion, didn't I?"

"Exactly what does that mean?"

"Woman trouble, sir. A man gets three stripes on
his sleeve and he begins to make a few promises he
can't keep. A change of station may be just the thing,
sir."

"I see." Early smiled. "All right, Sergeant, I leave
these details up to you."

"Yes, sir, I thought you would, sir. Likely I could
fill two squads with privates who'd take a transfer
over company punishment." He held up his hand as
Early opened his mouth to speak. "Oh, not mean
men, sir. Mostly just a little too much to drink, trouble in town, or cussing a corporal while under the
influence. The things a soldier does when he's on his

third hitch and those stripes are nowhere in sight."
He winked. "I know that the colonel will be culling
the guardhouse, sir, but if the captain will accept my
recommendation or—"

"I will," Early said. "And thank you, Sergeant."

Chapter Two

As soon as the retirement board adjourned, Gen. Adam Spencer took the first train back to Washington, for he missed the paved streets and the constant whirl of social life. The commanding officer of Fort Riley believed that his command enjoyed the amenities of civilization, and while Spencer was there, several important social events took place. The commanding officer felt that they were highly successful.

Adam Spencer did not. He thought that the regimental orchestra played badly and the ladies danced clumsily and they all had sweaty hands and there was not a decent unattached female on the post.

He was in a hurry to leave, but General Simmons and the others were not. Taking pack horses and shotguns, they spent three days on a bird-shooting expedition and loafed.

But a lifetime in the service rather limited their conversation, and the talk always swung back to military matters. They were sprawled around the evening fire and the sunset was making the prairie bright with color when Simmons said, "I'll have to head back in the morning. Paper is probably a foot high on my desk."

"You could have gone all week without reminding me of that," Kicheloe said. "But there's a loose end bothering me."

They looked at him. "What?" Nathan Buell asked.

"Well, we've activated five posts," Kicheloe said, "created twenty companies, and we've appointed no one to the position of responsibility for the whole thing."

"That requires a careful choice," Calhoun put in. "Nothing made on the spur of the moment."

"Exactly," Simmons said. "It would require a smart man to handle it. A difficult task—we all agreed on that. One where mistakes can be made."

"Many mistakes," Kicheloe said.

"Serious mistakes," Calhoun echoed.

"The man would have to be clever," Buell added.

"Yes," Simmons said. "Able to talk his way out of tough situations. 'Experienced' is the word I search for."

"Be difficult to find a colonel qualified," Kicheloe admitted. "Perhaps a general officer?" He let his eyes move from man to man. "Adam Spencer?"

"Oh, God, he'll scream," Buell said.

"I'd like to see it," Simmons said. "Letting him go all the way back to Washington and then hitting him with this. Is it right?"

"Poetic justice," Calhoun said, rising. "If we're agreed, I'll have the order cut over my signature."

"You'll make an enemy for life," Simmons warned.

Harvard Calhoun laughed. "Since when was he ever a friend? Of anyone?"

Lt. Joe Deacon and Lt. Harry Kitchen arrived on the same train, reported to the adjutant, and were immediately sent to the staging area where Capt. John Early was billeting his ever-growing companies.

Sergeant Deeter was recruiting and had already established a mess and stable area; he had two sergeants and four corporals and nearly fifty troopers, all eager to get out of Fort Robinson for one reason or another.

A pitched tent was Early's headquarters office, and two clerks kept the records. He was there, talking to Sergeant Deeter, when Deacon and Kitchen arrived, reporting in and handing Early their orders.

"Why don't we go to my quarters for a drink and a cigar?" Early suggested. "Sergeant, keep the lid on until I get back." He went out with them, steering them around the parade ground to Bachelor Row.

They stepped inside when he opened the door, and since there were not enough chairs, Deacon sat on the bed. Early got out his bottle and poured, then offered them cigars and a light. "Did you bring your son with you, Mr. Kitchen?"

The young man's eyes popped up like blue corks released in a bottle! they tilted up and looked at Early. "I—left him with a woman in town, sir. Bringing him on the post seemed ill-advised."

"Then I suggest you go get the boy. Sergeant Deeter will provide you with a horse. I'm sure he knows an enlisted man's wife who will care for him while you're on duty."

Kitchen had a smooth, almost beardless face; he seemed stuck with an eternal youthfulness, and at first glance a man would take him to be nineteen at most. He kept rolling his cigar between his fingers and shifting it from hand to hand. Then he said, "You're being very considerate, sir. I'm—not accustomed to it."

"If you don't like it," Early suggested, "why haven't you resigned your commission? Can it be that a man can love the very thing that rags him and makes him miserable?" Then he smiled. "Go get your son, Mr. Kitchen."

"Thank you, sir." He tossed off his drink, picked up his kepi, and walked out.

After his footfalls had faded down the walk, Joe Deacon said, "Well, John, it's, been six years. None of them really very good."

"They never promised us they would be when we took the oath." Early studied Deacon's face! it seemed more wan, thinner than he remembered, yet the man was still handsome; it was the kind of face a woman liked to see, rather square, symmetrical, with good eyes and a mouth that was a bit sensual. "I'm glad to have you with me, Joe," Early said.

"Are you really?" He laughed. "Then you're the first." He glanced at his cigar, got rid of the growing ash, and leaned back. "When I got my orders, I wasn't sure just what this was. Then the adjutant told me you were in command."

"Did that make a difference?"

He shrugged. "Well, John, I knew I was going to serve a man who'd been spit on enough to understand what it was like."

"You understand our function at Camp Sheridan?"

Deacon nodded. "I already figured it was something no one else wanted to do." He finished his drink and got up to put the glass on Early's dresser. "John, aren't you going to ask me about the major's wife?"

"No."

"Why not?"

"Because I don't give a damn one way or another."

Deacon said, "Suppose I swore to you that there was nothing to it, that I just took her to town so she could catch the train?"

"Swear anything you like," Early told him. "What difference would it make? I'm commanding a cavalry post, Joe, not a seminary for wayward men. Clear?"

"Yes, and it suits me just fine." He sighed and put on his kepi. "I like the assignment."

Fourteen days after his arrival, Capt. John Early had two companies formed, and Lt. Murray Butler arrived, taking his own time about it. He was a gnome of a man with thick glasses and a sandy moustache and a voice that bordered on a whisper.

He didn't give one whit about the assignment, and he had agreed to transfer to Camp Sheridan because he would be working closely with the Indians. Butler had lost all sense of military regulations; he never saluted anyone under any circumstances, and he forgot to say "sir" when spoken to. If he felt like donning a complete uniform, he did, but most of the time he didn't and wore whatever the laundry had sent back—usually a combination of blue and checked or striped shirts.

It was useless, senseless, and a waste of energy to require Butler to perform line duty; to have made him an officer of the day would have invited chaos, for his mind was on scholarly pursuits, and he was always writing and taking notes. He carried a wooden kit with him, and it had folding legs, and right in the middle of a walk across the parade ground a thought would come to him, and he'd set up on the colonel's grass and break out pen and ink.

All this irritated Col. George Barlow no end, and he summoned Captain Early to his office to talk to him about it. "I won't have this man disrupting the routine of the post!" Barlow roared and pounded the desk. "I don't give a damn who he is! No lieutenant is going to squat on my grass and write a lot of nonsense that only teachers will ever read!"

"I'm sure, sir, that Lieutenant Butler will be glad to hear your opinion," Early said.

"Opinion my foot! You're his commanding officer, and I'm ordering you to do something about it! That's all!"

"I'll see what I can do," Early said. He started to salute but stopped when the officer of the day charged in without knocking.

And before Barlow could vent his spleen against this horrible breech of conduct, the OD blurted: "Sir, Mr. Butler is sending smoke signals from the parade ground!"

Barlow came out of his chair. "With a fire?"

"Yessir!"

"ON MY GRASS?" He charged around the desk, rushed through the outer office, and took his first view from the porch. Lt. Murray Butler was indeed squatting on the parade ground; he had built a small fire on the grass and was sending up delicate puffs of smoke while about him stood a dozen of the ladies of the post, parasols erected against the hot sun.

Barlow and the OD, both quite fleet of foot, ran ahead of Early, who was hampered by his bad leg.

By the time Early arrived, Barlow was in a towering rage, demanding an explanation of this whole affair.

Still sitting on the ground before his fire, Murray Butler stared at the colonel through the magnifying lenses of his thick glasses. His brown eyes reminded Early of those of a rabbit, startled and alert, but not afraid.

Before Butler could explain—if he ever intended to—one of the ladies said, "Now, George, watch your temper in this heat." She had a wife's voice and a wife's tone that promised a lot of private trouble if this wasn't handled just right, and Barlow pulled back his displeasure and reconnoitered quickly. The other ladies, all wives of his majors and captains, stood solidly against him; he could feel it, like a quickly exhaled breath.

"But, my *dear*, a fire, on my grass, on my parade ground! What will people think?" He looked around and caught the OD's eye. "Haskin, get some water and put out that fire. My grass is ruined." Then he put his hand gently on his wife's arm. "Harriet— ladies—remember our dignity."

"Now don't start that, George," his wife said. "Mr. Butler was kind enough to demonstrate the Indian smoke signal, and, frankly, I found it instructive and very entertaining." She made shooing motions with her free hand. "So why don't you go back in your office and sign some papers, or whatever you do in there all the time?"

"Please, Harriet, people are watching us. Can't we disperse this gathering and discuss it later?" The OD returned with a bucket of water and doused the fire, leaving a charred, dark circle. Barlow looked at it, then closed his eyes for a moment; when he opened them, he looked at Capt. John Early. "Will you be so kind as to tell me when you're leaving the post?"

"By the end of the week, but I'm short a company."

"If you could march in the morning, I'll give you my word that I'll recruit another company for you," Barlow said. "But you must march with the command you now have. Understood?"

"Yes," Early said. "All right, sir, I'm as eager to leave as you are to—"

"I really think not!" Barlow snapped and chopped back across the grass to his office. The OD, having no further duties, left, and Early bowed to the ladies.

"My regrets that Lieutenant Butler's educational demonstration had to come to an end, but the colonel is quite sensitive about his grass. So if you'll excuse us, ladies?"

They thanked him and smiled and left, chattering and whirling their parasols, and Murray Butler got off the grass and brushed the seat of his pants. He said, "It was very good smoke, probably the best I ever made. Just enough green grass piled on to get good smoke. It's very difficult to get good smoke, John. For a long time I thought that all Indians could make smoke. Oh, I suppose they can, of sorts, but it takes skill to make good smoke. They have men in the tribe who are known for their smoke, just as we have good carpenters and saddle makers. Very interesting, isn't it? We're so eager to lump everyone in together, with common talents, that the habit sometimes trips us up."

"That's certainly true," Early said, taking his arm; they had to pause while Butler gathered up his writing box. Then they walked back toward the staging area. "But I wouldn't demonstrate any more. We'll be leaving in the morning."

"That'll be fine," Butler said. He walked with his head tipped forward, as though his vision were so poor that he had to concentrate heavily on the ground directly ahead of him. "Do you suppose any Indian saw my smoke? I was sending: 'Peace, Peace.' Rather a fitting and touching message. Actually that's a literal translation. The signal meant: 'Friend.'" He laughed softly. "I was taking poetic license, if you'll forgive me."

"In a few days we'll be on the reservation," Early said. "Feel free to go and come as you please. If you want someone to help you—"

"Perhaps I'd like one man," Butler said. "I am not as young as I once was, and someone to take care of the pack animals would be a genuine assistance." They stopped in front of Butler's tent. "I believe I'm going to enjoy my work with you, Captain."

Then Butler turned inside. Early looked up and saw Joe Deacon standing farther down; he walked on, and Deacon waited for him. "The old man put out the fire? Too bad. Someone's always coming along to spoil the fun."

"I want everyone ready to move tomorrow morning," Early said.

"We're short a company."

"That's right, but Barlow promised one."

Deacon shrugged. "You may never get it, and if you do, you may not want it."

"I think it's best that we get off the post," Early said. "I know the colonel is anxious, and so am I.

After all, I've never had a post command of my own, and I'm eager to get to it."

"They tell me it's ready to fall down," Deacon said.

"I'm sure there are no gardens growing. But we'll know soon. Have the companies ready to march an hour after mess call."

"That'll mean working half the night!"

Early stared at him. "What do you think this is—leave?"

Camp Sheridan was some fifty-odd miles to the northeast. Without pushing or dawdling, Early made it in two days and didn't wear out the horses to do it.

The post was situated on a creek, with a water gate opening right onto the north bank. The walls were log because timber was plentiful, but even half a mile away any man could see that the place was coming apart. The main gate hung askew, and weeds and grass grew belly high on the parade ground.

Early dismounted the command by the flagpole and detailed B Company, under Lieutenant Deacon, to see that the stables were put in good order without delay. Lieutenant Kitchen and his D Company were detailed to quarters and mess, the comfort of the enlisted men taking priority.

Since the captain had planned his march to arrive early in the day, they were left with nearly nine hours of daylight. All that day saws ripped and cut and hammers pounded, and by dark, when the cook fires burned brightly, visible signs of repair stood out; doors had been rehung and holes in roofs patched.

They had a week or ten days of work ahead before the post would be ready for inspection, but they would have that inspection, and every man knew it. A detail cleared the weeds off the parade, and another fixed the main gate by taking it completely off the hinges. All the upended logs making the palisade walls were pulled with an A frame; they needed new buildings, and this was quicker than cutting fresh timber.

There was no need for palisade walls, and an erected arch pointed out the main gate, and the logs taken down were quickly transformed into a quartermaster stores, a new line of stables, and a new enlisted barracks. Each company commander had his own headquarters, mess, and stable area, a luxury found only on the larger, well-regulated posts.

A central blacksmith shop was activated, and quarters for married officers, long fallen into decay, were repaired, cleaned, and painted inside, even though there were no married officers on the post.

Now the quartermaster supply train was due. Early and his command had been on the post for three weeks plus a few days. Camp Sheridan had already passed its first inspection, with eighteen men drawing extra duty and one corporal threatened with a bust if he ever exhibited a dirty carbine again.

The regulation day at Sheridan was sunup to taps; they were shorthanded, and John Early had no intention of altering his schedule because of it. He knew the time he had been allowed to activate the post, and he was determined to force some reluctant colonel to write up a glowing report because it had been done a lot sooner.

A signal wagon and crew arrived. They had been stringing poles, and in one day the signal sergeant announced that the key was in operation and that a five-man detail would be on duty at all times.

Captain Early sent a message: CAMP SHERIDAN READY FOR GENERAL INSPECTION.

Six words? The telegrapher was amazed, because these new commanding officers were generally pretty talky. But he sent the message, and, of course, Colonel Barlow was notified. He didn't believe a damned word of it; it was a lie, a bluff, because Early knew that it would be another thirty days before any general could schedule a visit. He's trying to make himself look good, Barlow thought, and fired a wire off to headquarters for permission to make an immediate preliminary inspection.

Confirmation and permission came back in a matter of hours, and he prepared to leave with the quartermaster wagons, which were starting out eight days late as it was.

Normally he would have hated the fifty-mile march, but anticipation of pinning Capt. John Early to the flagpole whetted his juices for revenge, and the miles passed unnoticed.

As they approached the post, Barlow was aghast to find that the palisade no longer stood, and he mentally rubbed his hands; he could really hit the roof over a thing like that. As they passed on through the main gate arch, Barlow noticed the new buildings and the company compounds and laid-out streets with packed clay marking the walks.

Early came out as the command went on toward the new quartermaster sheds, and as Barlow dismounted, Early saluted and had a corporal take the colonel's horse.

"Welcome to Camp Sheridan, sir. Come in and have a drink. It's been a warm ride, but we ought to get some rain one of these days.

He smiled and took Barlow's arm and led him onto the porch and inside. As he poured, he said, "I expect you'll want to inspect the post."

"Yes, I've been authorized by General Spencer."

Early turned quickly, surprised. "Spencer, eh? He's been given command?" He laughed softly. "Oh, he must be pleased about that."

"I'd watch my tongue there!"

"What for? What do I have to lose? Even you've said that I ought to have been retired years ago. As a matter of fact, the officers of this post really have very little to lose. So the general had best be cautious. And you might use some of it, George. Even as a plebe you were a pushy bastard."

"That's insubordinate!"

"Court-martial me," Early invited.

"I see you took the palisade wall down. By what authority?"

Early laughed. "George, you'll never catch me that way. Read your damned directives once in a while." He stepped to the door and spoke to the orderly. "Have Deacon and Kitchen here on the double."

The man ran out, and Early turned back inside and refreshed Barlow's glass. "I know why you're here, George. You want to catch me with my pants down. You're out of luck." He perched on the edge of his desk and eased his bad leg. "You're going to write one of your best reports, George."

"Am I?"

"You're damned right you are. And you're going

to initial my reports praising the efficiency and dedication to duty of Deacon and Kitchen."

Barlow grinned. "You're sure of that?"

"Positive." He looked around as Deacon and Kitchen came in, saluting. "White glove in fifteen minutes. All men full field. Rations for ten days' march."

"Yessir!" They said it in unison, did an about-face that was precise, and ran out, yelling to their sergeants.

Early and Barlow could see them out of the window, and Early said, "If you could have moved like that, George, you'd have graduated ninth in class instead of forty-fifth."

Barlow's eyebrow went up. "But you would still have been eighth?"

"Naturally," Early said, his manner pleasant. "You just never could pound the books hard enough."

"But I have a couple of eagles on my shoulder boxes," Barlow pointed out.

"Now you know I never gave a damn about rank. For me the service was enough. You want to know something? It is for Deacon and Kitchen, too. And Butler. One thing, George—you'll never be able to accuse any of us of seeking glory and promotion."

"You're right, but let me tell you something, John—you've never had a microscope turned on you as it is now. Every move you make will be watched and evaluated."

"That's not new. I found that out when I lost my eye. You commanding officers like your men whole, and even when we function on an equal with you, you suspect that something is wrong. Why is it that you're embarrassed when a man's scars show?" He held up his hand before Barlow could answer. "Remember Townsend? Grew long hair to cover that ugly scalp wound. And Carstairs took to wearing starched neckerchiefs to hide the scars on his throat. And what was that major's name, the one who wore gloves all the time, with two fingers stuffed to cover the ones he'd lost in the Comanche wars? You look at this patch over the eye, and the empty sleeve, and the limp, and you just know that I'm going to fail in my duty. And when I don't, you're angry because I've proved you wrong, and you hold it against me as though I'd personally set out to make a liar of you."

George Barlow nodded and looked at his boot toes. "Damn it, John, that's a pretty raw truth."

"Tell me I'm wrong."

"You're not wrong," Barlow said. Why do I do it? Can you tell me?"

"No, and I'm not sure I'd want to if I could." He got up and smiled. "Let's get on with that inspection, shall we?"

Chapter Three

Infantry troops generally stood barracks inspection with the soldiers at attention and the inspecting officer walking between them, alert for any breach of regulations. Cavalry stood inspection on the parade, each man holding his horse, and Col. George Barlow, with Early at his side and Sergeant Deeter behind them, his book and pencil poised, walked slowly before each company.

Lieutenant Deacon, commanding B Company, stood alone, his sergeant behind him, and because Barlow disliked Deacon, he gave the troopers a very close going-over and found only a few faults, which were duly noted.

D Company, commanded by Lieutenant Kitchen, got the same treatment. Nothing was perfect, and a few names went down in Deeter's book, but not many, and Barlow felt compelled to comment. "Captain, I notice quite a few visible bruises and a few black eyes. One man had a badly swollen nose. Can you account for this?"

Early passed the question to Deeter, who said, "Adjustment, sir. It's always difficult."

"I see," Barlow said, and they went on to inspect the buildings while the troopers were dismissed.

He took his time; he was looking for trouble, but

he found none. Even the unloading of the quartermaster supplies was orderly; the bales and boxes and barrels were being stored properly and inventoried as they went into the building.

The inspection ended at headquarters. Then they went into Captain Early's office, and Barlow took off his kepi and wiped away the sweat trapped there. He accepted the drink and cigar Early offered, then said, "You've suckered me into a good report, John. I should have known. Four years at the Academy should have taught me that you were a tactician." He puffed his cigar and smiled. "You mentioned some endorsements?"

"Yes, I have them right here," Early said and opened the door to speak to his clerks. "Will you bring me the reports on Deacon and Kitchen?"

When he turned back, Barlow said, "I didn't see Butler about. Is he out making smoke?"

"He went north to the reservation six days ago." Early smiled. "He was very anxious to get started on a book of Sioux music he's been working on."

George Barlow rolled his eyes. "What a ridiculous waste of time! I'll just never understand why the retirement board passes him over."

The clerk came in with the reports, and Early gave them to Barlow to read. The colonel frowned and pulled at his lip, then laid them on Early's desk, picked up the pen and affixed his signature.

"No argument, Colonel?"

"Not this time," Barlow said. "But I'm a patient man, John. I can afford to be. I'll give you a good report on your work so far, but you've just reactivated the post. Wait until you start digging into the mess at the reservation. I don't think you're going to know where to start."

"I haven't studied the situation so I don't know, either," Early said frankly. "Perhaps you'd be kind enough to send me any file you—"

Barlow laughed and shook his head. "Go take a look yourself. You won't believe it." He pointed his finger. "And when you deal with the agent and his assistants, please remember that you're dealing with civil servants, men appointed by powerful Washington politicians who will be easily offended and complain bitterly to General Spencer, who in turn will not be kindly disposed because he's lost his desk job and will be serving God knows how long on the crude frontier."

"That all sounds so cheerful," Early said. "When are you going to send me a surgeon and medical staff?"

"I was hoping you wouldn't mention that."

"Regulations, George. I'm entitled to one, you know."

"All right, I'll find someone who's looking for a change." He got up and picked up his gloves and kepi. "About that company I was going to—"

"That's all right," Early said. "In twenty-some years I've learned not to take your promises too seriously."

Color came into Barlow's face. "Why, damn you!" Then he calmed himself. "I suppose I deserved that because I meant to raid every guardhouse from the Dakotas to Texas. All right, John, I'll send you C Company, Lt. Phil Ewing commanding. They're a good company, so take care that they come back to me the same way. Ewing's got a career ahead of him. I'd hate to see that jeopardized by another man's failure."

"You think we'll fail, George?"

"Hell, you were sent here to fail! Now if you'll excuse me, I'll go to my quarters and get some rest."

John Early called a meeting in his office just before the noon mess, and he included Sergeant Deeter and two company sergeants. There were chairs enough only for the officers, so the sergeants stood. Early passed cigars all around.

"First, I want to congratulate you on the way you carried off the inspection. Against his will, Barlow signed my reports commending all of you." He glanced at the sergeants. "When are you going to learn to hit a man in the belly where it won't show?"

"Well, sir," Deeter said, "we did. You just saw the ones who needed more persuading."

"I see. So far I've kept out of troop discipline, leaving it all up to you. Now I want your frank appraisal as to how much trouble we're going to have."

Sergeant Myer, D Company, shifted his feet. "Sir, speaking very bluntly, the men think this is a rotten job, and they willingly transferred in to escape punishment or something, but now they think they went from the frying pan into the fire."

"Maybe they're right," Early said. "Gentlemen, I don't have to paint a picture. Most of us are here because no one thinks the job can be done, yet someone has to try, so they figure were just the ticket to try and then be thrown away. The rumor's probably around that General Spencer is in command of the agency posts, and he'll be sore because he got aced out of his

Washington post. Now there's a hot poker shoved at us, and I'm not going to get branded by it, and neither are you, so you are going to perform duty in a manner more exact than you have ever performed before. The man who fails me isn't even going to know what fell on him. Clear?"

They nodded.

"Now, point two," Early said. "You sergeants are going to have to perform the duties of second lieutenants; we're short of officers and likely will be because Barlow will do us no favors. In the future, and by that I mean from this moment on, all infractions, big or little, by an enlisted man will be handled by me right here in this office."

The sergeants showed surprise because this had never happened to them before; tradition dictated that a commander refrain from in-ranks discipline. Deeter said, "Sir, although I did my best, most of these lads are a bit fractious, sir, if you know what I mean. I'm trying to say that the captain will be spending half a day every day just taking care of—"

"I predict that it won't last long," Early said, his manner blunt. "Gentlemen, I don't think a man is long out of recruit barracks before he is aware of just how much authority a sergeant or corporal has. Then you give him a couple of hitches under his belt and some 'bad' time and a post like this where we're short three officers right away, and he'll figure he can kick the flagpole any time he feels like it." He looked at Deacon and Kitchen and saw that they agreed completely. "I want both of you to take a good look at your troopers and advise me of any you think can carry the responsibility of promotion. Frankly, my

motives are selfish. A corporal long overdue for ser-
geancy is inclined to back the officer who kicked
him upstairs and definitely inclined to keep a tight
rein on his squad because he wants to keep his
stripes."

Joe Deacon asked, "Captain, can you get authori-
zation to promote these men?"

Early shrugged. "Well, a post commander has some
latitude there, Joe. I can promote and then fight it out
with headquarters, if General Spencer ever decides
where it's going to be." He looked around. "Any questions?"

There were none, so he excused them and spent
the rest of the afternoon in his office working on an
organization table. He had two clerks, both young
and inexperienced men on their first hitch, and he
had Sergeant Deeter, who was trying to be sergeant
major and first sergeant at the same time, and no
man could be both, or either well, for one demanded
that he be all over the post constantly and the other
that he remain in the headquarters office.

Deeter would have been Early's choice, but he
couldn't demote the man; he had to search for someone else. The clerks brought in the personnel records, and he went over them and found a corporal
in B Company who had been a first sergeant but had
been broken and court-martialed for involvement in
a payroll robbery twelve years before. He had been
acquitted, but his rank had never been restored.

His name was McKeever, and Early sent a clerk to
fetch him. He came in, a tall man near forty, with a
red face that would never tan and a precise, military
manner.

"Stand at ease, McKeever." Early tipped his chair back. "I've been looking at your record. Would you care to say anything?"

"I figured you'd get around to it, sir. Every officer does sooner or later."

"I see that Colonel Barlow gave you the bust. Can you tell me why he didn't restore your grade after the acquittal?"

"No, sir, but if the captain knows the colonel, he doesn't need an answer to that."

"That's right, I don't. You're a man with a high school education, McKeever. I need a first sergeant, and I'll give you the same chance we're all getting— one shot at the target. They're waiting for us to make a mess of everything, but we're not going to." He looked at McKeever steadily. "If you understand that and want the job, you can take charge of your duties and move into your quarters in this building right away."

"Thank you, Captain. And if you'll pardon a little noise in the outer office for a day or two, I'll get those clerks to get into the proper work position—butt up and head down."

"Very good, Sergeant. Write up the order and I'll sign it. That's all."

News of a promotion passes fast through a post for it starts a chain reaction; there are only so many grades to a company, a command, and the elevation of one man means that his grade is vacant and someone is going to get it.

By the time the quartermaster supplies were unloaded, Captain Early had made three sergeants and seven corporals. This meant two days of careful screening of records and listening to recommendations, for the quartermaster teamsters worked very slowly, liked to start late and quit early. Early took advantage of this to get Colonel Barlow's signature.

When he came to Early's office, Barlow said, "I know what you've been doing, John. Damn it, you're taking advantage of me, and you know it."

"If the colonel wishes to protest, I'd be glad to appeal to General Spencer. Surely you're not going to deny me an adequately rated command?" He smiled and shoved the orders across the desk. "This is a small thing, George. Tomorrow you'll be going back, and what I do here won't bother you a bit. None of this is your responsibility." He moved the pen closer to Barlow's hand. "In all the time we've known each other, you've owed me a few favors, and I've never asked for any of them."

"I can't sign McKeever's order! Hell, I busted him in the first place!" He looked steadily at John Early. "You know, you remember too damned much. Some things that a man did fifteen years ago ought to be forgotten."

"Oh, they are, George, unless a man is forced to remember. I know that woman meant nothing to you. A harmless flirtation, that was all. But I could also see how it could have been misunderstood." He waggled his finger. "A check, George, of all things. Cash would have been more suitable for a woman who neither toiled nor spun."

"Let me have that damned pen," Barlow said, and endorsed the orders for promotion. "But this squares us, John. I don't want to ever hear of it again." Then he laughed. "Harriet is rather narrow-minded about some things, John, and a man's loneliness is really beyond her comprehension." He got up and drew on his gloves. "Would you believe me if I wished you luck?"

"Yes. I never thought you were a mean man, George. A little selfish where your career was concerned, but never vindictive." He heard a small commotion in the outer office and flung open the door, surprising Sergeant McKeever, who was about to knock. "Yes, Sergeant?"

"Sir, I wish you'd come out. Lieutenant Butler has returned, and he's very upset. He has some Indians with him."

"I'll be right along," Early said and reached for his cap.

Colonel Barlow was looking at Sergeant McKeever; he said, "I'm glad to see you've regained your grade, Sergeant. I hope you understood that under the circumstances I couldn't—"

"That's all right, Colonel." McKeever turned and went out with Early.

Butler was in the middle of the parade ground, he had five Indians with him, and as Early hurried over, he thought that they were the poorest-looking Indians he had ever seen. Their clothes were castoffs—rags, really—and they were lean as well-run hounds.

"Ah," Butler said, grabbing Early's arm and clinging to it. Behind his thick glasses his eyes watered endlessly, and he kept sniffing. "Captain, because I doubted that you would believe the despicable conditions at the reservation, I brought along these poor souls as witnesses. They speak fair English and understand it well. However, I'd be glad to translate if you—"

"Thank you, Mr. Butler, but I think I can manage. Yankton, are they not?"

"Yes," he said. "Sir, do I have your permission to have them fed? They came only because I promised they'd be fed."

"Of course. McKeever, have them taken to the mess and tell the cook—"

"I know what to tell him, sir."

The Indians didn't want to go, but Butler spoke to them softly, and they turned and followed McKeever. "Oh, they're pitiful—indeed, I know of no other word to describe things, Captain. They have no shelter worth mentioning and no food and—"

Early was looking past Butler to the horses they had ridden in. "Mr. Butler, you left with enough supplies to last a month, and your pack horses are—"

"I gave away everything I had," Butler admitted; he grabbed Early's arm again. "I spoke to the officials at the reservation headquarters, and one man threw me out."

Colonel Barlow, who had kept out of this so far, said, "Bodily?"

Butler looked at him, squinted as though he had just discovered he had been standing there. "Who are you? Oh, yes, I remember. You have a delightful wife, very intelligent. How is your grass?"

"Damn the grass! Were you speaking literally or figuratively?"

"Oh, literally," Butler said, and promptly took off his shirt and peeled down the top of his underwear to show Barlow the immense welts across his back. "I was bruised when I fell on the porch steps. He was a big man, of course, or I'd have given him a better fight. But I lost my glasses in the scuffle and—"

"Mr. Butler," Early said, "I suggest that you get a bath and a good night's rest. I'll ride back with you in the morning." He put his hand on Butler's shoulder and gave it a gentle shake, for he was dealing with a gentle man. "You're an officer in the United States Army, Mr. Butler, and we won't have our officers knocked about. Now get some rest. We'll put your friends up for the night and fill their bellies."

"Thank you," Butler said and walked away, his head bent forward, studying the ground ahead of him.

"Pathetic little man," Barlow said, and then seemed uneasy when John Early stared at him. He turned then and walked away.

Sergeant McKeever came back and joined Early. McKeever looked after the colonel briefly, then said, "The Indians are being fed, sir. Anything else?"

"Tell Lieutenant Kitchen I want to see him in my office in twenty minutes."

He answered the sergeant's salute and walked slowly back to headquarters, feeling a rising anger, but an anger directed at no one in particular. A man could feel anger at circumstance and situation and because no one cared he felt that way now, and it was odd to be worked up because some Indians were being starved to death. It was not a feeling born of affection for the Indian; Early had, every time he looked in a mirror, a solid reason for hating them, but the warriors who had inflicted his terrible wounds were dead, killed by his own hand, and it was done with. A man could not hate them all for what was done honorably in battle.

Lieutenant Kitchen reported a few minutes early; he was a prompt, exact officer determined to perform his duty in a flawless manner. As soon as he swept off his kepi and tucked it under his arm, Early said, "Close the door and sit down, Mr. Kitchen. Did you see the Indians Mr. Butler brought back with him?"

"Yes, sir. A pretty ragged lot."

"A man can get dirty without wanting to, and he can reduce his clothing to rags and not mean to, but he won't go hungry unless he's made to. I've never seen more downtrodden Indians, Mr. Kitchen. They have no spirit at all. In the morning, after mess call, I want you and a picked squad to accompany me to the Pine Ridge Agency. We've been sitting here on our butts, Mr. Kitchen, and it's time we go have a look. If things are as bad as I think they are, we'll have to do some housecleaning and straightening up."

"Very well, sir. Do you want to leave before the colonel departs or after?"

"I'm not running my command for the colonel's pleasure," Early said. "He arrived without ceremony, and he can leave the same way. That will be all, Mr. Kitchen. I leave the details to you."

"Yes, sir." He got up and turned to the door, but stopped there when Early spoke.

"Now and then I think about your son, and as soon as we return I think you should make some arrangement to have him here with you. When children are small, they just don't understand separations from their parents."

"There's no one to take care of him, sir. That's why I left him in—"

"Yes, yes, I understand. But we should find someone, Mr. Kitchen."

"Thank you, sir. I'll do what I can."

After Kitchen left, John Early walked a few doors down to the quarters Colonel Barlow occupied; he knocked and heard Barlow's permission to enter. The colonel was stretched out on the bed, and when Early came in, Barlow sat up reluctantly.

"What is it, John?"

"I'm sorry to have intruded on your rest, sir, but I'd appreciate any information you could give me on the personnel at the agency." He smiled wryly. "Reports and files and information haven't exactly deluged my office, sir, and I haven't been briefed on the situation at all."

"Damned simple to explain—no one really knows what it is."

"Have you been to the reservation?"

"Yes. Seven months ago. General Calhoun ordered me to make an inspection." He waved his hand. "How in hell does a man describe it? I don't think he can, because we are not familiar with terms that characterize the filth and poverty."

"Who is in charge?"

"Mr. Earl Grover. His father is a Senator from Michigan. Very influential man. He has an assistant, Dan Marley. I don't know anything about him except that he and Grover work well together. Unless I miss my guess, Marley is the man who roughed up Lieutenant Butler. He has the size for it and the disposition." He reached into his tunic pocket for a smoke and lit it. "John, I'd be very careful there. You'll be dealing with a man of influence and—"

"George, you really must develop a more flexible attitude if you expect to get on in the service. Now if I were an ambitious major due for a promotion, I'd be quite careful, but I'm not. I'm a captain long frozen in rank, and I don't have a damned thing that Grover can take away from me."

"He can get you retired damned fast," Barlow snapped.

"George, wasn't this to be my last assignment, anyway?"

The colonel held his eyes for a moment, then gnawed at his lower lip while he nodded. "All right, John, go ahead and do as you want to—you will, anyway. If you weren't such a damned maverick, you'd be a colonel now in some foreign attaché's office, charming the ladies with your dueling scars."

"I rather think I'd like that," Early said, surprising Barlow.

"You're joking!"

"No, I'm serious. I speak French, you know." He laughed. "Wouldn't that be the bitter end, though? Some soft post in Paris, writing a few dispatches and watching someone else's army sweat on maneuvers?"

"You'd hate it."

"Fifteen years ago I'd have hated it," Early said. "Maybe even five, but it gets more attractive as time goes on."

Barlow studied him at length, then said, "John, I swear I'll never really figure you out at all."

"Yes," Early told him, "it must be hell not being able to make up your mind whether you like me or not." He put on his kepi and turned to the door. "Thanks for the advice."

"I meant it as a warning. John, you won't like Earl Grover, and he won't like you on general principles. But it's useless for me to tell you to be careful; you never were. You damned heroes!" He laughed softly. "You know my views. There is really only one way for an officer to fight, and that is perched on high ground, viewing the battle through field glasses. He then lives to fight again."

"That's an older man's philosophy. Good-bye, George, and give my best to your wife. I'll be off the post before you leave in the morning." He opened the door, then gave Barlow one parting shot. "If you happen to communicate with General Spencer, tell him I'm going to raise holy hell."

"He'll appreciate that," Barlow said sarcastically. "As the officer in command, the responsibility will fall on him."

John Early laughed. "George, between you and me and the fence post, it's about time something fell on General Spencer. To my knowledge, he's the only general in the army who has never heard a shot fired in anger. I don't think he ever qualified with a pistol."

"Shall I tell him you said that, too?"

"I think he already knows it," Early said and closed the door.

Chapter Four

In a changing world an Indian agency was something that did not change, because change required effort, and this was a fulcrum rarely applied by agents. Land was set aside for Indian use, usually poor land that no one ever wanted, and if time proved the land to have some hidden value, then the Indian was always moved off it to another agency.

Capt. John Early had accumulated considerable experience with Indian agencies, beginning in Arizona in the mid-'70s with the San Carlos Apaches and carrying on through to his ride north to Pine Ridge.

Harry Kitchen commanded a picked squad, with Sergeant Rafferty as sergeant in charge; Rafferty was a new man, recently promoted from corporal and eager to demonstrate his ability to handle the rank. Behind the squad rode Lieutenant Butler and his Indians. Butler kept taking off his glasses to wipe dust off them; he could easily have ridden to one side or at the head of the column, but he just didn't think of it.

Fifteen miles separated Sheridan from Pine Ridge, and Early held them to a steady march and arrived a few minutes after nine o'clock. Early dismounted his detail near the flagpole, turned the whole thing over to Sergeant Rafferty, then walked with Harry Kitchen toward the headquarters porch. The building had been built at government expense, which meant sawed lumber hauled a hundred miles and carpenters brought in to build it. The shingles were made of tarred composition, and the whole thing had been given several coats of gray paint.

As they mounted the porch, the door opened and a large man stepped out, a huge smile breaking across his face. He extended his hand and said, "I'm Dan Marley. You must be Early."

They shook hands briefly, and Early said, "I'd like to speak to Mr. Grover."

"He's not up yet."

Early made a show of consulting his hunting case watch. "At eight minutes after nine? Is the man sick?"

"No. Mr. Grover likes his rest." He smiled, then looked past Early and saw Lieutenant Butler talking to some Indians over where the trooper was holding the horses. Marley's pleasure faded, and he said, "What the hell's he doing back here? I thought I made it plain—"

"Ah, yes," Early cut in. "Since you've introduced the subject, I want to discuss this with you, Mr. Marley. We just can't have officers of the United States Ar—"

"That old fool? I don't consider him anything. Hell, he came barging in while Mr. Grover was having his lunch and made all sorts of insane demands."

"And you threw him off the porch," Early said.

"That's right. What of it?"

"Throw me off the porch," Early invited.

Marley looked at him, then laughed. "Are you crazy? What for?" He watched John Early, and his laughter ebbed. "What are you trying to start here, anyway?"

"You already started it when you manhandled

Mr. Butler," Early said and reached out and started to thrust Marley out of the way. And when the man reacted, Early reversed his push and suddenly yanked Marley forward and tripped him so that he took the flight of eight steps in a loose roll. He hit hard, grunted, and then sat up and looked around, trying to get his bearings.

Early said, "Sergeant Rafferty, please see that this man remains outside while I talk with Mr. Grover."

"Yes, sir." Rafferty looked at Marley and doubled his fist. "Get up if you want. I ain't had a good fight since payday."

Early went on into the building, Harry Kitchen following him. He stopped inside and looked around, at the rugs on the floor and the ornate table lamps and good furniture that had come unscratched all the way from Omaha.

Kitchen spoke softly. "I've never seen a general's quarters, but it must be like this."

Early had completed his inspection. "And where is the prince of this castle? Look around, Mr. Kitchen."

Kitchen crossed the room, opened a few doors, and Early continued his examination of the furniture. There was a large grandfather clock in one corner of the office, and a large mahogany bookcase with a glass front.

Then a man yelled, "What's the meaning of this!" and Early walked over to the last door Harry Kitchen had opened. He looked in and found a man in bed, a breakfast tray before him.

"You are Mr. Grover? Agent in charge?" Early asked, smiling, approaching the bed. "I'm Capt. John Early, commanding Camp Sheridan. This is Lieutenant

Kitchen, commanding D Company. Isn't it a little late to be having breakfast?"

A girl hurried in; she had heard Grover's yell. She stopped just inside the door and looked first at Early, then at Kitchen. She was perhaps eighteen, and she was slender and very graceful. Her hair was a light brown—some women would have coaxed it a shade lighter and claimed it blond—but her eyes were brown, and they marked her as having a trace of Indian blood in her.

Grover said, "Jean, hand my robe to me, and show these gentlemen out. Take the tray. I'm quite finished."

The girl nodded and started to him, but Early put out his hand gently. "Mr. Kitchen, will you see the young lady back to the outer room? I'll assist Mr. Grover with his toilet."

"Now see here—" Grover stopped because Kitchen and the girl were already out and the door was being closed. "Captain, I resent this high-handed manner! Where is Mr. Marley?"

"He's being entertained by one of my sergeants," Early said, lifting the tray off Grover's knees. His head brushed the lace canopy on the bed, and he drew up a frail chair and sat down. "My, you're certainly living in splendor, Mr. Grover. I was particularly impressed by the rows of whitewashed rocks skirting the flower garden and flagpole. Do you have the water carried to keep the plants green? I only ask because I've had a bit of experience with parade ground grass, and I'm interested in a green lawn. Show me a post with a green parade, I always say, and I'll show you a tightly run post." He ran his finger over some of the furniture and found no dust. "Remarkable cleanliness, Mr. Grover. But of course you have servants. A gentleman should, you know. I consider it quite improper for a man of breeding to cook and care for himself. Don't you?"

Grover was watching Early intently then he sighed and smiled. "I must say that Im very relieved, Captain. From your entrance I thought you were going to be—difficult." He laughed and clasped his hands together. "I have never seen a more miserable place. This building, these rooms—they are an oasis of comfort in a pitiless desert of filth and heat and dust."

"I quite agree," Early said, rising. "But I must allow you the privacy of dressing. I'll wait for you in the outer office." He pointed to the first room they had entered. "That expanse of opulence does suffice as your office, doesn't it?"

"Yes," Grover said. "I'll join you in a half hour." He saw the question in Earl's expression. "My bath, Captain, my bath."

"Of course. How thoughtless of me." He smiled and bowed slightly and went out, and the moment he closed the door, his expression hardened.

He found Kitchen in one of the pantry rooms, talking to the girl Grover had called Jean. Early said, "Mr. Kitchen, would you be so kind as to commence an audit of the agency books?"

"Right away," Kitchen said and went out.

The girl looked at Early, looked at the patch over his eye, and his pinned-up sleeve, then she said, "The Sioux call you Many Deaths. I've heard them talk about you many times."

"Are you part Sioux?"

"My grandmother was Sioux. It's a long story, but I was raised by them. When my mother died, my father didn't know what to do, so he brought me to the village. I was raised by them."

"Why do you stay here? This job?" He lit a cigar, scratching the match on his thumbnail. "How many servants does Grover have?"

"Six in the building. About twenty to carry water and do outside work."

"And you get paid?"

She laughed. "Captain, there's no pay. You get food. You won't have to ask anyone who works for Mr. Grover. Just look around, and when you see an Indian with meat on his bones, you'll know."

"Thank you. You've been very helpful."

He went back through the front of the building. Harry Kitchen had the record books open on the desk and was concentrating on them. Early stepped out to the porch and found Sergeant Rafferty checking a nosebleed and squinting through an eye that would be closed by nightfall.

Dan Marley sat on the top step, leaning his back against a porch upright, a bloody handkerchief pressed to his mouth. Blood streaked his face and soiled his white shirt front, and Early saw two bloody teeth in the dust. Marley's eyes were badly puffed, and his nose looked broken.

Sergeant Rafferty came to attention and said, "Everything's under control, sir."

"Yes, I can see it is," Early remarked. "Did Mr. Marley fall, Sergeant?"

"Yes, sir, and I grabbed for him and fell myself, sir. Very clumsy of me, sir."

"Indeed," Early said dryly. "But you fell quietly enough. Carry on, Sergeant."

"Thank you, sir."

Early puffed his cigar and then turned and went back inside. The girl was bringing some coffee to Harry Kitchen, and she got another cup for John Early.

"I neglected to ask your name," he said.

"Jean Stillwell."

"You speak very well."

"Yes, I went to school at the Standing Rock Agency. Then I spent two years studying nursing in Council Bluffs. She smiled. "Why am I here? My foster mother, Captain. She's old and dying, I think. I owe her that. The food I've earned here has kept her alive for a long time. Did you want to know anything else?"

"No," he said. "Please leave the building. If there are any others with you, take them out, too." He saw the question in her eyes and answered it. "There is no more work here until further notice."

"And no more food."

"I didn't say that. Please go now, and thank you for the coffee."

She was turning to leave when Earl Grover stepped out of his bedroom. He wore a fine brown suit and a stickpin in his tie, and his attention was immediately caught by Harry Kitchen, at *his* desk, going through *his* books.

"Captain, what is the meaning of this? Jean, tell Marley to come in here immediately!"

"Mr. Marley is occupied," Early said mildly. "He's sitting on the porch, if you'd like to talk to him."

Grover hesitated, then flung open the door. He took one look at Marley, let out an alarmed bleat, and slammed the door. "Captain, I'll have you thrown out of the army for this!"

"Perhaps, but that will be preceded by my throwing you out of the Indian Service. I have seen enough and heard enough already to convince me that you have misused government funds and supplies. Please consider yourself under arrest."

"I'll do nothing of the kind!"

Early shrugged and went to the door. "Corporal Adams, please come here." He held the door open, and the corporal came in. "With drawn pistol, corporal, I want you to keep Mr. Grover under close guard. If he attempts to escape, shoot him in the foot."

"The foot, sir?"

"Exactly. A man can run with a .45 in his thigh, if he's desperate enough, but he won't go far without a foot. Now take this man out and follow my orders."

Earl Grover started to protest, which was a mistake, for he failed to understand that a captain's order to a corporal was excuse enough to get cuffed around a little if one turned unruly. The corporal shoved and applied his boot to the bottom of Grover's expensive pants and propelled him through the opened door. Then Early closed it, blew out a long breath, and said, "Harry, we're going to get into a lot of trouble now. What do you say?"

"Can we fight, sir?"

"Yes, with weapons they never thought we had," Early said, then took off his blouse and joined Kitchen at the desk.

To free the sergeant and corporal from guard duty, Grover and Marley were locked into a stout storeroom, and with McKeever as company, Early began an inspection of the locked supply buildings. A search failed to turn up a key, so Early ordered Sergeant McKeever to shoot the locks off, which he did with a .45-70 carbine.

The place was packed with issue flour, beans, sacked corn, salt—all the staples that should have been issued to the Indians.

There was no time for an inventory, and Early did not intend to take one. He summoned Lieutenant Butler and told him to see that the word was spread around the reservation that there would be a food issue on the parade ground and for the Indians to bring sacks and buckets and anything they had to carry it in.

Jean Stillwell was located, and she brought all the Indians Grover had been using for servants, and Sergeant McKeever gave them all the food they could carry; it was the best way to advertise that a ration was getting under way.

That evening, even before sundown, they began to come in, in pairs, in families, some halt and blind, and all painfully thin. The soldiers ladled out the flour and corn, and they kept it up by firelight all through the night.

Early stayed with them until ten o'clock, then he went inside and drew up a chair by Grover's desk. Kitchen was still at the books and had half a tablet full of figures.

"Sir, I don't think you're going to believe this at all."

"Try me," Early urged.

Kitchen had his tunic off and his sleeves rolled up. Then Jean Stillwell came in with coffee and sandwiches. Early said, "I thought I told you to—"

"I know what you told me, Captain," she said, cutting him off. "I'll stay because I don't think you're the kind of man that bothers to look after himself." Then she went out and closed the kitchen door.

Harry Kitchen grinned. "That's quite a girl, Captain." Then he turned back to the work he had done. "I think I've figured it out, sir. I've made an incomplete list of supplies that have come into the reservation this last year. Eighty barrels of flour, nine ton of salt, thirty-five ton of potatoes, a hundred barrels of sugar, sixteen ton of dried—"

"Wait a minute. The government paid for all this?"

"Yes," Kitchen said. "And you've got starving Indians? Hell, sir, they should weigh a couple of hundred pounds apiece. Now I don't know where the stuff has been going, but the Indians didn't get it, and all of it still isn't in the supply house. I'd bet on that."

"You'd win," Early said. He offered Kitchen a cigar, then lit one for himself. "It seems to me that we must move fast, yet our great danger is in moving fast. Ten hours from the time we release Grover, he'll be sending a telegram and pull all hell down on our heads."

"Why release him then?" Kitchen said. "Can't he be our guest for a month or two? Surely through the summer. It's the best time of the year."

"That would mean that we would have to send in reports in Mr. Grover's name, Harry. Do you think that's quite honest?"

"Well, as honest as his has been. He's falsified the text and signed his real name. We'll send an accurate text and falsify the name. That sounds like an even swap to me."

"Harry, if we're caught, we won't stand a chance at a court-martial."

"Who gives a damn?" Kitchen said.

"All right, we'll go ahead. But I think straightening up this deal Grover has going—whatever it is—won't be enough to take the heat off. There's one thing that even a politician can't buck and that's public opinion, Harry. Every time the ax is whetted, we'll have to come up with something that stays the hand."

"Put ourselves in a position where they don't dare land on us?"

"Exactly."

"That's some problem," Kitchen admitted. "Maybe I should have listened to my father and stayed in the newspaper business."

John Early's head came up; he speared Kitchen with his good eye. "What did you say? Your father owns a newspaper?"

"Sure, back in Canton, Ohio. I put in my apprenticeship there and—"

"By God, you've got it! We're going to put out an agency newspaper. Write your father a letter—now, tonight—I'll send it out with a trooper. Telegraph is too risky, and I don't want anyone to know about this until it's too late to do anything about it." He slapped the desk. "Make a list now. Everything you need to put out a two-pager with pictures. Get a camera and plates and developers and all the things we need and have them shipped out as—textbooks. Warn your father to do it quietly." He got up and started to limp around the room, massaging his thigh. "We're due for rain; this leg has been giving me a fit all day."

"My dad likes a fight," Harry Kitchen said. "He's sixty, but he'll still scrap. If I told him what we were up against—"

"Go ahead," Early said. "That stuff ought to be here in two weeks if he ships it right away. That might give us time to find out what the hell is going on here and who's been getting all the rations intended for the Indians."

"There's a direct telegraph line between here and Fort Robinson, sir. The key and batteries are in that closet over there. I found them by accident when I was looking for some scratch paper." He looked curiously at Early. "Do you think Marley knows how to operate it?"

"It would be my guess. Grover doesn't strike me as being patient enough to learn code. Do we have anyone who can work a key?"

"Corporal Adams put one hitch in the Signal Corps," Kitchen said. "Sir, I don't mean any disrespect, but if that line to Fort Robinson is so damned private, then—"

"I was considering that, Harry." Early pulled at his moustache. "We'll sit tight on it awhile and see if anyone makes a signal. You'd better have the corporal assigned here so he can be handy. Until we know whether or not Colonel Barlow is working something on the side with Earl Grover, we'd just better see what we can do for the good of the Indians." He went to the door to throw away his cigar. "And while I'm thinking of it, it might be a good idea to get the men out of uniform and into anything they can find in the supply house that fits."

"I'm afraid I don't unders—"

"Harry, before you have anything to sell, what do you have to have?"

"A buyer."

"Fine. Now who's the buyer?"

"Don't know."

"Neither do I, but it might be someone who'd be scared off by the army." He winked. "Get some sleep. I'll stay up until the wee hours, then you can relieve me."

"Where's Lieutenant Butler?"

"Singing songs with his Sioux friends probably," Early said and stepped out to the porch. The rationing was still going on by the supply building. Lanterns cast yellow puddles of light around, and the crowd of Indians there had not thinned out.

Jean Stillwell spoke from the dark shadows. "Some of them have come back the second time because they can't believe it will ever happen again."

"That's all right," Early said and walked over to her. "You're pretty stubborn, aren't you?"

"Yes, I am. Aren't you?"

"Too much, so I've been told."

"There are going to be men who are going to be dreadfully sorry you were given this duty," Jean Stillwell said. "When the colonel from Fort Robinson came here, I thought he would change things, but he didn't. He had the telegraph wire installed. Marley knows how to make it work."

"Are you sure about Colonel Barlow?"

She peered at him carefully. "Is he a friend of yours?"

"We were at West Point together. I've known him many years."

"I see. Then I shouldn't expect too much, should I?" She looked at the Indians near the supply building. "Perhaps they're right—this may not happen again."

"Don't you have any faith in anything?" he asked.

"Well, it isn't easy," she admitted. "But from the first moment I saw you I began to have it. I told myself that here was a man who long ago had nothing more to lose as far as the army went. It's in your face, Captain. You've carried that carbine around with the last shot in it so long that you just can't wait to fire it. You're going out and you know it, but you want to go out with the ground shaking and the limbs falling off the trees and the stars doing dip-ups. You'll go, but in the big thunder. Right?"

"Right. Where I go isn't important because I'll have no regrets."

"None?"

"Well, one or two, but not concerning the army."

"Tell me about them," she invited.

He laughed. "They're rather personal."

"What isn't, really? I'm a good listener."

He hesitated, then said, "I regret that in my earlier years I didn't seek a wife. Perhaps with a home, children, the prospect of being out of the army wouldn't seem so bleak."

"You're not actually in your dotage," Jean Stillwell said. "If you looked around—"

"No, no," he said quickly. "It's not my looking around that governs the situation. A woman—"

He was making her angry, and she let him see it.

"Are we talking about a woman or some simpering slut with powder on her cheeks? An empty sleeve, a patch over one eye doesn't frighten a *woman*, Captain."

She was pinning him to the wall, taking away his armor, his comfortable excuses, and he didn't like that. "I wear this patch not as an affectation but to cover an ugly sight. An Apache knife—"

"Why don't you show it to me and frighten me, make me pale, and prove that you were right all along?"

He looked at her a moment, then took off his kepi and the band from around his head. She said, "Turn so the light shines on you." He did, slowly, giving her a chance to retreat, but she did not. She put her hands on his shoulders and pulled him down and examined the damage the Apache's knife had done. There was no paleness in her cheeks, no trembling of the warm fingers gripping him.

Then she said, "That must have hurt you terribly."

She let him go, and he straightened and put the patch on again. She kept watching him, her expression serious. "Perhaps you're thinking that it's because I've lived with Indians and seen ugly things. I don't think so. I saw ugly things in Council Bluffs. An eyeball deadened by a knife isn't a thing that would frighten me." She tapped his chest. "It's the things in here, the things I can't see that frighten me."

Then she turned and walked off the porch, going toward quarters she kept across the parade ground. He watched her until the night swallowed her completely, then he wondered what excuse he would use now, what balm he would dip into to ease the loneliness that all single men must sooner or later feel.

She took something from me tonight, he thought, and lit another cigar.

Chapter Five

Gen. Adam Spencer chose Fort Laramie for his headquarters, not because it was centrally located, but because it was an old post and had many established comforts. And it was on the railroad, which meant that he did not have to endure any mounted travel of any great distance.

The post commander, a colonel of severe yet just tendencies, did not exhibit any profound joy when he learned that he would have a general on the post. The commander was not worried because of any irregularity in his command, but generals always make colonels a little nervous; it's a matter of principle.

It took General Spencer several weeks to get situated; he had furniture to move, and mementos collected along the track of his career, and he insisted that his quarters be painted anew and clerical personnel be provided in an office adjoining his quarters.

Then there was a round of parties and teas to host; this took another week; it was almost a month before he got around to telegraphing his post commanders for full reports of their activity.

There was Major Andress at Fort Yates, near the Standing Rock Agency. Major Cohill commanded Fort Custer near the Crow Agency, and Spencer sincerely hoped that he would never have to go there, for Montana, from all reports, was a most miserable place. Lieutenant Colonel Jahns commanded Fort Sidney near the Pawnee Agency, and Captain Early Camp Sheridan.

Since Fort Robinson was on the railroad, General Spencer took the train and threw Colonel Barlow into a panic by arriving on the post unannounced. The country was in the middle of a rainy spell, and the post was at a slack time and certainly not ready for any general to look around. By the time the OD told the colonel that General Spencer was on the post, the general was already making his way into headquarters and Barlow had him rushed right into the office.

"General, this is a most pleasant surprise. Please sit down. A whiskey, sir? A cigar?" He laughed. "Perhaps not one of your fine panatelas, but—"

"Very cordial of you," Spencer said, accepting the drink and the cigar. He puffed as Barlow held the match. "I've established my headquarters at Laramie. A wonderful post. Full of tradition and all that sort of thing." He patted his stomach and smiled. "Frankly, I find it good to be on the frontier. I've always wanted to serve here, you know, but one damned duty or another kept me chained to a desk." He chuckled. "That's the price one has to pay for having a mind keen on logistics and strategy."

"Yes, indeed, General. I've always envied you your administrative ability." He hesitated, then went behind his desk and sat down. "May I ask the purpose of your visit? An inspection in this weather wouldn't be practical, sir. Even if the rain lets up, we'll be ankle-deep in mud for a week."

"No, no, nothing like that," Spencer said quickly.

He arched back in his chair and elevated his head as though terribly conscious of his profile; he liked to turn his head partially when talking to people, treating them to the classic mold of his chin and nose. "As you know, sir, my position is one of grave responsibilities, and my commanders are not—like yourself—men without limitations. Given a choice, I would cashier the lot and replace them with responsible officers, men of proved dedication."

"Yes, I understand, sir," Barlow said. I had Early and his—his group here. That damned old fool, Butler, made smoke on my grass."

Spencer looked at him as though he had just confronted a man who had lost his mind; Barlow decided not to push that line of conversation too far. I would be interested in looking over any communication Early sends you, Colonel. By that I mean, simply send on to my headquarters any—"

"I understand, and I'll be happy to," Barlow said. Is there any way in which I can assist the general?"

Spencer regarded him carefully. "You don't like him, either."

"Sometimes I think I do, then I believe I don't," Barlow said. "The general can rely on me in all matters."

"I'm sure I can, sir." Spencer used "sir" frequently. It was more condescending than respectful, but no junior officer could object to it. "I found the report of your inspection and recommendations waiting for me. It's difficult to believe that he could have activated the post that quickly. But it's no matter." He drew on his cigar, then screened himself behind a momentary haze of smoke. "I did not endorse the commendations, and I am not going to enclose them in their folder. This is not a disrespect of your judgment, sir, but a reservation I hold in my mind concerning this whole thing. Early and the others were foisted on me, against my will and against my judgment, by General Calhoun and General Simmons. I'm going to prove them wrong, sir, and when the next board convenes, I'm going to be chairman of it." He let Barlow digest this for a moment. "Has Early put in an appearance at the reservation?"

"Yes, sir. Nearly ten days ago. I sent Mr. Grover, the agent in charge, a telegram a week ago, and he reports that he and Early have reached a mutual understanding in the administration of the agency." He leaned forward and spoke confidentially. "General, I can assure you—no, I can promise you that you will have no trouble at all from Captain Early."

"Exactly what does that mean?"

Barlow smiled. "The general must accept my guarantee, but I can assure you, sir, that you will be entirely pleased."

"God, I hope so," Spencer said, blowing out a long breath. "These agencies are an abomination, and there's no sense denying it. Some newspapermen from the East toured a few three years ago, and some of the politicians think they can cull votes by raising a smell. I want the dust sprinkled, Barlow—that's all I ask. Just a little oil spread on the troubled waters."

"General, with Captain Early in complete accord with Mr. Grover, you can achieve your wish. It is as sure as the sun."

"You sound very confident, sir."

"Completely, General." Barlow got up. "Now, may I make arrangements for a dinner tonight, honoring your visit? Perhaps a dance afterward? The ladies on the post would most like to meet you."

Corporal Adams moved into the agency headquarters because he could operate the telegraph key and his services were needed to respond to a telegram from Colonel Barlow. The colonel was concerned about Earl Grover's relationship with Captain Early, but a telegram sent in Grover's name assured the colonel that all was amiable and that a spirit of complete cooperation existed.

John Early had worded the wire carefully because he was groping in the dark and didn't know what he was going to bump into. He found out three days later when a quartermaster detail arrived with five wagons and a sealed dispatch from Col. George Barlow.

There was some difficulty getting the quartermaster lieutenant to give up the dispatch to anyone—he had orders to deliver it personally to Earl Grover—but Early finally convinced him that Grover was on agency business and wouldn't be back for three days. The lieutenant was free to wait, of course, but—he decided not to and gave the dispatch to Early.

When Early read it, the light went on and the picture took on new color and detail. He called Lieutenant Kitchen, who came in wearing an old canvas coat and a checked shirt. "Move the wagons over to the supply buildings and load these supplies."

Kitchen looked at the order, and no flicker of surprise crossed his face. "All right," he said. "Take a couple of hours." He went out and slammed the door, and Early offered the quartermaster officer a drink.

The lieutenant was not at ease; he kept twirling

his kepi in his hands and moving his feet. Early said, "Don't be nervous. You're under orders, aren't you?"

"Yes, sir." He took the whiskey and tossed it off. "But I don't like it, sir. I can say that, can't I?"

"I may not like it myself," Early said, but what can I do about it? Mr. Grover is a government agent, and if he chooses to divert supplies and equipment to Colonel Barlow, how can I stop him? What I want to do doesn't enter into it, Lieutenant." He sipped his whiskey. "Of course, the sutler must be making money; he gets supplies for nothing and sells them for full retail, taking on freight charges." He held up three fingers. "Mr. Grover's share. Colonel Barlow's share. And the sutler's share."

"And each man must make his own arrangements," the lieutenant said flatly. "Mr. Grover must settle with you, sir."

"That's very insubordinate, isn't it?"

"Prefer charges if you want then—sir."

John Early smiled. "I'd rather keep this dispatch, Lieutenant."

The officer looked up, surprised, and a bit suspicious. "The colonel expects me to bring that back, Captain."

"Tell him you forgot it. If he wants it bad enough he can telegraph me, and I'll conveniently 'find' it, and in a few days or a week I'll send it back with a dispatch rider."

"Why do you want to do that, sir?" He put his glass aside and sat straight in the chair.

"I might be able to make a duplicate of it."

The lieutenant sat for a moment, studying John

Early. Then he asked, "Where is Mr. Grover? And don't tell me he's on the reservation. He'd be here—he always is. He's not the kind to ride a horse just to look after Indians."

"He's under close confinement," Early said softly. "Locked up. He sees no one, talks to no one except the guard. Marley is also confined."

The lieutenant smiled. "Keep the dispatch, sir. I'll think of something to tell the colonel."

"Don't get yourself in trouble," Early warned. "I may need you for other duties."

"Sir, I'm sorry for what I said—"

Early waved his hand. "If you hadn't said it, I wouldn't have told you what I did." He got off the edge of his desk and walked around the room, limping at each step. "Mr. Prine, a captain does not accuse a colonel without evidence. I must gather that, and carefully. Do you understand? In no way must the colonel suspect that Mr. Grover is not in charge of the reservation or that we are not cooperating in the fullest. I expect that Barlow will question you about me. Convince him that I've inspected the reservation and can see that nothing really can be done. Assure him that I've come to realize that my military career is drawing to a close and that I intend to sit out this assignment and make no waves to rock the boat. These, of course, cannot be told as admissions; a captain wouldn't confide that much in a second lieutenant. They will be your impressions, gleaned from my conversation and actions. Do you understand?"

"Yes, sir. I do."

"Fine. Now don't let your conscience be further

disturbed. We'll cause a large row one of these days, and you'll be needed to testify."

"I'll testify," Prine said. "And gladly."

When the wagons were loaded, Lieutenant Prine left the reservation without delay and Harry Kitchen came to headquarters, his manner agitated. Before he could say anything, Early handed him Grover's dispatch and said, "Get on your horse and ride over to Hot Springs and get the newspaper to take a picture of this. Bring back the print *and* plate. He'll want to keep the plate, but don't allow that. You ought to be back by dark tomorrow. Sometime tomorrow I'll wire Barlow that I found his dispatch where I had misplaced it and will send it to Robinson by messenger. That will calm his fears and buy us time to get a copy made." He shook his head. "I certainly wish that shipment from your father would arrive."

"I'm sure he's sent it, sir." Kitchen said and carefully put the dispatch inside his tunic. "It's clouding up for rain, and the flies are biting like fury. I'll be off the post in ten minutes."

Actually he shaved a few minutes off that prediction. John Early watched him go, then walked over to the storage room that served as cells for Grover and Marley. The soldier there unlocked the door, and Grover blinked at the rush of light. He was unwashed and unshaven. There was a cedar bucket half full of water.

"You dirty swine," Grover said. "I'll have you in prison for this, Early."

"Oh, I don't think so. I sent three wagon loads back with Lieutenant Prine."

Grover stared, swallowed, then said, "I—I don't understand. Why didn't you arrest them?"

"Now that would be stupid," John Early told him. "Hell man, I think you have a good thing going here. I'm just cutting you out of it, that's all."

"Wait! We can work together! Let's talk about it!"

"No talk. Look at me, Grover. I'm on borrowed time as far as the army is concerned, and a man can save only so much on a captain's pay. If I'm going to retire, then I'm going to do it in style. How much can I make here in one year? Thirty thousand? Probably more."

"What are you going to do with me?"

"Aren't you comfortable?"

"There are mice in here!"

Early laughed. "I'll get you a cat then. Close the door and lock it, soldier."

Grover started to yell and pound his fists, but it did him no good, and he quit it. To the soldier, Early said, "If he starts to raise a commotion, you have my permission to rock him to sleep. You have no compunctions about hitting a civilian, have you?"

"None in the least, Captain."

Early found Sergeant Rafferty at the supply building; he was keeping an exact inventory of everything that had been withdrawn. "Tomorrow," Early said, "I want you to pick a man to return to Robinson with a dispatch, but I want him to stop off at Sheridan and have Sergeant Myer bring a platoon to the reservation."

"All right, sir, but that'll make us very shorthanded here."

"It will only be temporary, sergeant; Mr. Kitchen

will be back by tomorrow night, and Jean can cook until Myer gets his detail here. Have you seen her?"

"She left when the wagons showed up, but I expect she'll be back."

The sound of horses approaching drew them to the door. Four men were crossing the parade toward headquarters, and Early walked to join them there. They were cattlemen, with wide chaps flapping and pistols belted to their hips, and they went right on in. When he stepped inside, they had already helped themselves to the whiskey and cigars.

They looked at him, and one said, Where's Grover?"

"He's on the reservation. I'm in charge until he gets back."

"We'll wait," the man said.

"It'll be several days," Early told him. "Of course, you're welcome to stay, Mr. —"

"Cal Ormond. I ranch west of here." He looked steadily at Early. "Are you sure he won't be back before—"

"Quite sure. He and Marley left yesterday and rode north. There'd been a knifing. Some Indians got hold of some whiskey and—"

Ormond laughed. "Hell, I know how that is. How come I never saw you here before?"

"I've been here only a short time. What can I do for you gentlemen?"

Ormond looked at the others, then said, "I brought you some cattle. A hundred and fifty head of two-year-old heifers." He took a bill of sale from his pocket and handed it to Early. "Fifty dollars a head."

John Early studied the bill of sale, then said,

"Mr. Grover didn't authorize me to pay out any money."

"Hell, we can't wait until he comes back," Ormond said testily. "Give me my half, and we'll be on our way. Look, he sent for me—I didn't come here on my own."

Early understood then that there were no cattle and never would be; Grover got the bill of sale and paid Ormond half the stipulated sale price and pocketed the other half for himself. "I'll get the money," Early said and stepped outside, casting his glance about quickly for anyone who was handy. He saw two troopers standing near the end of the building and pointed to the cattlemen's horses, waving violently away. The soldiers got the idea, gathered up the reins, and led the horses out of sight behind the old stable.

Early walked to the far end of the porch, drubbing his mind for some kind of answer—a quick answer because Ormond was not stupid and would soon know that he was being dangled. The safe was in the office, and if Early had gone for money, he would have walked to the corner of the room and opened it.

But he couldn't do that because he didn't know the combination.

He trotted to the guard and had him open up; he ducked inside, placed the flat of his hand against Grover's face and banged his head once—and hard—against the wall. "Tell me the combination of the safe and I won't ask you again," Early said in a voice that was soft and dangerous. "Damn it, tell me or you'll never see outside this door!"

The suddenness, the fright of it all made Grover

speak before he had a chance to think it over. "Seven left, fifteen right, nine left, and twice to zero," he said. "Are you going to release me now?"

Early was dashing out, and the guard locked the door. Then he dogtrotted back to headquarters, and as he rounded the corner he saw Cal Ormond and his men come to the porch and scowl.

"Where the hell's our horses?" Ormond asked, his hand never far from his pistol. "What the hell's going on here, anyway?"

"I had your horses watered," Early said. He smiled disarmingly. "I had the combination of the safe written down, and I had to get it. You all seem a little nervous."

"We just don't like to hang around," Ormond said. He pointed to the south, where a company of cavalry approached in a neat column. "Now get the money so we can get out of here."

"Certainly," Early said and went inside and knelt by the safe. The approaching column would undoubtedly be Lieutenant Ewing and C Company, and Early wondered what he should do—let Ewing walk into something he didn't understand, or give Ormond the money and let him get out.

He missed the combination at the first try and Ormond rapped him impatiently on the shoulder. "Come on, come on!"

"I'll get it," Early said, his manner apologetic. "I just haven't worked the safe many times, that's all." He twirled the dial, cleared the lock, then began again, this time succeeding. He opened the door and began to count out the money, and he could hear the cavalry getting closer, hear Ewing's commands as the company halted on the parade and dismounted.

"Let me have that," Ormond said tightly and grabbed the box. He quickly counted out seventy-five hundred dollars and turned as Lieutenant Ewing mounted the porch.

He came in, a precise young man, tall and erect, his quick, intelligent glance going over them. He focused on Early and said, "Ah, Captain, although we've never met, I recognize you. May I present myself—"

"Captain?" Ormond roared and swung around, drawing his gun.

Early's hand went across his body, and he met Ormond's turn, bringing the long barrel of his pistol crashing down. And as Ormond wilted, spilling money across the floor, Early eared back the hammer and halted the others halfway through a bit of fatal foolishness.

"Mr. Ewing, I'm delighted to see you," Early said. "Would you please relieve these gentlemen of their weapons and have them taken outside and placed under close guard?"

"Yes, sir." He saluted correctly.

It took a few minutes to clear the room, and Early picked up the fallen money, returned it to the box and the safe. He closed the door, spun the lock, but thoughtfully wrote down the combination on a slip of paper for future reference.

Lieutenant Ewing came back; he was curious but would not think of asking any questions. Early poured him a drink. "Did you bring a full company, Mr. Ewing?"

"Yes, sir. I'm detached to your command, sir."

"That," Early said, "must have been a disappointment." He looked at the young man and smiled. "You can be frank and honest with me. That's the way we are around here."

"To be honest, sir, I would have preferred other duty. But I intend to give you my best, sir, and the best from my men. No man will ever note in my record that I shrank from anything."

"Well said, Mr. Ewing. But what you have believed to be a dull and listless assignment is going to prove to be quite challenging." Early crossed to the window and looked out. A squad guarded the cowboys, and Cal Ormond was coming to, holding his head and looking a little sick to his stomach. Early turned his back on the window. "Mr. Ewing, you have ridden across a portion of the reservation, and you may have noticed the conditions of filth and squalor. In short, the reservation is a mess. I placed the agent in charge and his assistant under close arrest, and I've taken over. That, Mr. Ewing, is a fact that we are not going to disclose to anyone at the present time." He waved his hand to indicate the men now under guard, then he handed Phil Ewing the bill of sale. "You noticed no cattle as you rode in? There were none, yet this bill of sale was given to me, and some simple arithmetic gives you a rather considerable figure. Top market value and then some, wouldn't you say?"

"Yes, I would."

"The deal between Mr. Ormond, who now has a sore head, and the agent, who rests under lock and key, is that Ormond supplies a bill of sale for the records and Grover supplies the cash, half to Ormond and half in Grover's pocket, while in the books money was paid out, cattle received and, of course, issued to the Indians." He smiled thinly. "You can quickly gather the nutritional value therein."

"The bastards!" Ewing said.

"You grasp the picture very quickly," Early said. "Please sit down, Mr. Ewing. Would you like another drink?"

"Thank you, no," Ewing said. "Sir, I'm surprised that Colonel Barlow hasn't learned of this and sent a company here to clean it up."

Early studied him—the gray eyes and the neat, sandy hair and the moustache valiantly trying to bloom to sweeping proportions. "Mr. Ewing, you strike me as a sincere, dedicated young man. Tell me, are you fond of the colonel?"

"Yes, sir. By that I mean I'm fond of him because he is my commander and a man should respect his commander."

"I see," Early said. "Do you believe then that a commander is above reproach because he must be respected?"

"I—I'm not sure I understand that, Captain. If I may speak frankly, I've heard that you're a real maverick, sir, but that you are widely respected for your devotion to duty, your integrity, and your personal courage. And I have served under a commander who had my respect as a military man, yet I detested him for personal reasons."

"Then let me put it another way: where does your real loyalty rest, Mr. Ewing? In individuals or the honor of the service?"

"Captain, I chose the army, and I worked like hell

to graduate twenty-sixth in my class. I've always wanted to be a soldier, and my loyalty is to my oath. Meaning no disrespect, sir, but I'd personally charge you, in spite of your record and your Medal of Honor, if I knew you had betrayed that oath." He glanced at his fingertips. "You will learn it from my record, so I might as well say it now—I served as aide-de-camp to Gen. Adam Spencer for nearly a year, and I asked for a transfer because I couldn't reconcile myself to the general's methods. Ask any man in my company, sir, and he'll tell you that I go by the book and I'll brain any man with it who tries to step outside it."

John Early got off the corner of the desk, rubbing his leg because it pained him almost constantly. "Mr. Ewing, I'm delighted to have you here. Please settle your company, then move your gear into the spare room. You'll billet here with myself and Lieutenant Kitchen."

Chapter Six

Lt. Harry Kitchen returned to the reservation with the original dispatch and two copies, and Early locked these in the safe without telling Lieutenant Ewing any thing about it.

Early seemed to be drowning in details. There was the matter of having a stone guardhouse constructed; he had put Lieutenant Ewing and his men on this, and work was progressing satisfactorily. Jean Stillwell had returned to full-time work in the headquarters building, and Early had reached a salary agreement with her and the eight Indians she had brought with her. They kept the cooking chores for the soldiers out of everyone's way, took care of the laundry and the horses—all constant duties that a soldier put up with when he was off his permanent post.

A wire from Lieutenant Deacon informed Early that a surgeon and three corpsmen had arrived at Camp Sheridan, and Early wired back, ordering the surgeon and two of the corpsmen on to the reservation. Many of the Indians were sick. There was no doctor available, and Early had no faith at all in the medicine man.

Paper work was a loathsome thing to him, and he had mounds of it. Supplies had to be ordered and re-ordered constantly. From the account books Early put together a more complete picture of Earl Grover's enterprises. All the ordering was done on government vouchers, and the merchant merely filled the order, presented the voucher, and got his money. It was a beautiful way to get rich, because it allowed goods to be sold without prior inspection and to be received and signed for without actual inspection by the one who paid the bills.

A merchant in Sioux City supplied everything to the reservation—food, hardware, coal oil, everything—and Early noted that the goods was always shipped from the railhead through the same freight company.

All of which smacked of a deal. But it was a deal Early did not understand, so he played it very cautious. Using old orders as examples, he made out a new one and carefully traced Earl Grover's name on it.

An independent freighter arrived with his wagon, and it contained four crates of educational material. These were carried inside and put in a spare room, and Harry Kitchen immediately began to uncrate and assemble the printing press, while two others set up the fonts of type and tables.

To satisfy Lieutenant Ewing's curiosity, Early told him that the reservation was going to publish its own newspaper, chock-full of tribal news and items of ethnological value. Lieutenant Butler would act as editor, and the whole project should prove very interesting.

In four days the doctor completed a partial swing of the reservation and reported back to John Early: he could not recall worse conditions, and this included experiences in a Confederate prison camp in his youth. The Indians needed beef, and they weren't getting it. They were meat eaters; it was their main fare, and they had to have it because they would not change their habits or learn how to prepare other foods.

Early had no way of knowing when the last beef had been issued, and he questioned Jean Stillwell about it. She thought that it had been sometime in the fall; she couldn't remember exactly. The records showed that enough beef had been issued to fatten every Indian on the reservation.

It was just another problem that had to be taken care of right away. He had no idea where beef could be bought, although there were ranchers around the reservation. Grover had bought, at least on paper, from several, and Early couldn't be certain which of them or if all of them worked with Grover.

The problem was still with him when a deputy sheriff rode out and introduced himself as Miles Candy; he was looking for Cal Ormond and three other cowboys who had disappeared about nine days before. Ormond's wife, suspecting that he had run off with another woman, had instigated the search. Early, with a completely straight face, denied any knowledge of the man.

No, Mr. Grover was out and wouldn't be back for a few days.

Yes, he'd tell Mr. Grover.

The deputy was a cordial man; when he went out to his horse, Early went with him, and they chatted about how much good the recent rain had done and the fact that it looked like a generally hot, dry summer. Early turned the conversation deftly to beef and remarked that he certainly hoped Ormond came back because he needed beef badly.

On that note the deputy rode away and Early returned to his own mounting worries. He was skating where the ice was thin, trying to turn lies and deceptions into facts, and he was sure that he couldn't get away with it for long. Either Colonel Barlow would show up or something would happen to tip the balance and send it all sliding into disgrace before he could accumulate his forces to oust the whole lot.

Harry Kitchen was spending a lot of time in a darkroom he had made out of a closet. He patiently photographed each page of the account book and all other records he could slip under the camera. And in his spare time he was trying to put together the first issue of the newspaper. Lieutenant Butler wanted to include some Sioux music, and he was hurt when Kitchen refused; Butler just did not understand the purpose of the paper and believed that it was going to be distributed only on the reservation.

Lieutenant Ewing believed that also, but for entirely different reasons.

A woman came to see John Early; she was tall and slender, in her thirties, and she had two young sons with her. She rode like a man and dressed like a man, but as she dismounted, Early observed that she would never pass for a man.

She came directly to him, extending her hand. "I heard that Grover was away for a few days and that you needed beef."

"You talked to the deputy?"

She nodded. "He came to my place looking for

Ormond and his friends. That was stupid and a waste of time. If Ormond or any of his kind ever set foot on my place, he'd get shot." She put a hand on the head of her older boy. "This is Ken. That's Bill. Bill's twelve, but he looks older." She smiled at Early, and her glance touched his eye patch and empty sleeve. "Say, you've been knocked around a little, haven't you? You must be pretty tough to keep coming back for more."

She had a rather angular face, very pleasant, with good eyes and full, expressive lips and a nose that was as straight as any he had ever seen.

"I'm Capt. John Early," he said.

"Stella Parish," she said. "I've got nearly two hundred head I'll sell."

"Fifty dollars a head?" he asked.

"Good Lord! This is scrub, Captain. I had eighteen dollars in mind."

Early bowed. "My apologies, madam. I should have known by looking."

"Known what? That I'm not a crook like Grover and Ormond?" She shook her head, and her braids swished against her shoulders. "I've sold Grover cattle for years. He's a dirty little worm, and I get rid of scrub that way. I have no love for Indians, Captain. They killed my husband. He was a soldier, a corporal. But I didn't come here to talk about that."

"When can you deliver the cattle?" Early asked.

"Late tomorrow afternoon. You can tally at the corral and pay me afterward. They're wild as ticks, Captain. Pretty scrubby. They need a summer to fatten, but I haven't got the hands to manage it."

"You've made a deal," Early said. "Would you like

to come in? I'll get the cook to make some coffee and fix a meal."

"I didn't come to put you out," Stella Parish said.

"Please, it would be my pleasure."

They went inside, and the boys went over to the soldiers' barracks. Early went briefly into the kitchen and found Jean Stillwell there, and she promised coffee in a few minutes. Stella Parish was looking around the office when Early came back. She said, "He sure likes to live high on the hog doesn't he?" She turned and looked at John Early. "I'll bet this rubs you raw."

"Why do you say that?"

Her shoulders moved in a shrug. "A man like you just has to be honest. It takes something like principle to hold a man up when the road gets rough."

"You've got a few bruises from the bumps yourself?"

"One or two," she said. "But no one's complaining. I own my own place, and somehow I manage to end up each year with a few dollars left over." She studied him frankly. "Captain, where *is* Earl Grover?"

"I told you—"

"I know what you told me, and I don't believe it. He wouldn't leave this office to look at an Indian if he had gold teeth. Grover's not away any place. And I think you know where Ormond and his bunch are."

"The deputy was satisfied that I—"

"Oh, hell, he's bucking for sheriff next election, and he wouldn't dream of offending anyone. He'd believe you if you told him the moon was made of cheese."

"You're a very perceptive woman, Mrs. Parish. I've

got the whole lot of them locked in a stone guard-house I had built back by the creek."

She stared a moment, then laughed heartily. "Oh, that's wonderful! Really wonderful. May I look at them? I'd like to see Grover behind bars, just once."

He shook his head. "That's not possible, I'm afraid. I think he should be in jail, but not laughed at."

"Of course you're right," she said quickly. "That was a thoughtless thing for me to say." She turned as Jean Stillwell came in with a tray. When Jean put the tray down, Stella Parish said, "You've done your hair different Jean. When a woman does that, it means that—well, it really doesn't matter."

"Stay and have some coffee," Early suggested.

Jean Stillwell shook her head. "Mr. Kitchen wants me to help him. It's nice to see you again, Stella. Will there be anything else, Captain?"

"Thank you, no," Early said and watched her go. Then: "You know her well, Mrs. Parish?"

"Call me Stella. Yes, for some years. She's a good girl. Too bad a decent man can't see it. But she's a quarter blood, and they just can't forget it." She poured her coffee and added sugar. "Your name keeps sticking in my mind. I'm sure my husband spoke of you to me. You were with General Miles, weren't you?"

"Until I got shot off my horse," Early said. "I just have never learned to duck properly." He laughed and took a cigar out of his pocket and held it up, making the question with raised eyebrows, and she shook her head, telling him that she didn't mind if he smoked. After he got his light, he said, "You realize that I've laid open both flanks to attack by telling you what I have. A word from you and it would all be lost."

"You know I won't talk," she said. "You knew it right off, Captain."

"Yes, I judged you correctly," he said. "Stella, I've been going over all the papers in Grover's desk, and I've come across a bundle of letters written by his father."

"And how is the dear Senator, the dirty crook? All right, I'm guessing, but like father, like son. Unfair of me, isn't it?"

"Yes."

"But I'm permitted to have prejudices, am I not?" She watched him nod. "Good. I just can't like a man who denies a woman everything."

He laughed because her frankness delighted him. "Tell me why you haven't remarried. You're a very attractive woman."

"In jeans and a cotton shirt?"

"Jeans and a cotton shirt can't hide everything." He watched quick color come to her face, but she wasn't offended.

"I guess it was a fair question," she said. "John, I married one man because I loved him and he was a good man. The second one would have to be better, and I just don't think I've run into one yet. I'm thirty-four and I've already put a charge of bird shot into the seat of one man's pants who couldn't get it out of his mind that all widows are lonely. That, quite naturally, brought out a certain shyness in single men, so I really can't say that I had a chance to judge them all fairly. And I've got two sons. That is considered a handicap."

"It wouldn't be to me," John Early said frankly. "Of course, I'm speaking in generalities."

"Naturally," Stella Parish said. "But if you were ever inclined to speak in particular, I don't expect you'd be shy about it."

Jean Stillwell came in and announced that dinner was on the table, and Early took Stella Parish into the dining room. Lieutenant Ewing came in and was introduced, then Lieutenant Kitchen came in and was surprised to find a strange woman sitting beside him. He recovered and was gracious through the meal.

Murray Butler didn't come in for his dinner, but no one paid any attention to that because he was always off somewhere, pursuing some personal quest for knowledge that no one seemed to be particularly interested in.

Dr. Mulvahill came in late and apologized for it; an Indian woman had been having a difficult time in childbirth, but he was happy to say that everything had gone off all right. Mulvahill was in his fifties, a grave man who took medicine too seriously; he brooded constantly over the many he could not help or save, and he wrote all this down in a thick diary and composed countless articles for the medical journals.

"I was wondering," John Early said during a lull in the conversation, "if any of you gentlemen are accomplished in forging?" Their heads came up as though jerked by a common string. "I'm trying to come to terms with a problem before it actually arrives. The mail courier arrives twice a month; he's due any day. In going through Mr. Grover's files, I find that he has corresponded regularly with his father and also gets letters regularly from his father. The problem is going to be to answer the communication that's going to arrive any time."

"That's going to be sticky," Phil Ewing said. "I'd be willing to practice, sir. I got all A's in mechanical drawing, and I have an eye for art."

"We'll give you a chance then," Early said. He sighed and revealed how deeply he felt this trouble. "Gentlemen, time is running out for us. We cannot keep Grover and the others locked up indefinitely, regardless of how closely he is guarded. More and more people know the truth, and the danger is thereby increased by the rule of squares. Harry, how close are you to running off the first issue?"

"It's going to be four pages, sir. Two more days."

"Can you cut that down a little?"

"I need some more help, sir. Jean's been working with me, but—"

"My boys could go back alone," Stella Parish said. "I'd be glad to help."

"That's very kind of you, but to involve yourself—"

She cut John Early off. "Listen, I was involved two years ago when I called Earl Grover a dirty little crook to his face."

"Thank you," Early said. "We'll accept. Now, the situation, although grave, is growing clearer and therefore more easily defined in terms of defense. In the morning I want to send a wire and ask for Lieutenant Prine's services. I want him here for a week or ten days, and I think Barlow will consent to that without having his suspicions aroused. Harry, you ought to be able to get those papers printed and off by Friday. I want every editor of every major newspaper to have one. With documented evidence responsibly presented, many of them are bound to make a front-page story out of it." He looked around the table. "Needless to say, we'll all be court-martialed, but a public row is exactly what we want. It's like trying to shoot with one charge a whole covey of quail. If we go after Grover alone, his father and Barlow and the others will scatter. So we have to—"

"Pardon me, sir," Ewing said, "but that's twice you've mentioned the colonel's name."

Early looked at him. "Mr. Ewing, it pains me to tell you this, but we can prove that Colonel Barlow has been drawing supplies out of this warehouse, transporting them with quartermaster wagons to the sutler's store at Robinson, and selling them there, with the profits divided according to an agreement previously set with Grover."

The color seemed to drain from Phil Ewing's face, and he looked quite ill. Then he composed himself and said, "You have proof?"

"Complete."

Ewing looked around before speaking. "I gave you my opinion some time ago, captain. Nothing has happened to change that."

Lt. Murray Butler was disappointed when he read the first issue of the Pine Ridge *Enterprise* for it contained not one line of Sioux tribal music or paragraph about smoke signal communication; he felt that it had no ethnological value at all, and he was right.

The paper contained accounts of illnesses and one whole column of death notices and the causes—pox, pneumonia, malnutrition, and in some cases starvation.

It included Dr. Mulvahill's report, nearly a half page of narrative description of living conditions, sanitation, and the health situation, and the article included three excellent photographs taken by Harry Kitchen. The best, John Early thought, was one of a small, naked Indian child sitting in the dirt in front of the most miserable and poorly constructed lodge; Early could not recall ever seeing so hopeless an expression on the face of a human being.

On the opposite page there was a six-photo layout of the headquarters building with the lavish interior display and Early thought this was a clever thing for Harry Kitchen to have done—to contrast the two this way.

The front page was attractive looking, and the banner was a woodcut, well done. The quality of the work made Early wonder why Harry Kitchen wanted to stay in the army when he could do work like this. The first page was devoted to Earl Grover's management of the agency and the way he manipulated and pocketed government funds. Early was certain that editors would read this paper, and if they featured the report about Grover, other papers would pick it up, and the explosion would be heard from Washington to San Francisco.

Early was satisfied, and the papers were bundled, and Harry Kitchen, in the company of a corporal and two troopers, left the reservation for the railhead at Yankton, where the papers would be addressed and mailed out to the newspapers. Kitchen had a list supplied by his father, and he and Early had gone over it, selecting the major papers.

Stella Parish's beef arrived and was turned into the

corral, and Early had Lieutenant Butler pass the word that there would be a ration immediately and that every grown male Indian who was the head of a family was eligible to receive one steer. Early paid Stella Parish in cash from the funds kept in the safe, for he suspected that soon he would be under arrest and that the agency funds would be frozen and that anyone holding script would have to wait for his money.

He didn't want that to happen to her.

Sergeant Deeter and a detail arrived from Camp Sheridan; he had Lieutenant Kitchen's small son with him, riding double, which was a treat for any boy. Jean Stillwell promptly took the boy in tow and won him with a smile and a kiss and a tour of the kitchen, where she promised to bake him some cookies.

Early introduced Deeter to Stella Parish. Deeter nodded politely, then gave Early a thin leather dispatch case. "Thought I'd better hand-carry these, sir. All from General Spencer. He's set up headquarters at Fort Laramie, sir. A blessing to the post if there ever was one, sir."

Early smiled, saying, "Now that wasn't at all necessary, Sergeant. True, but not necessary." He tucked the dispatch case in his belt. "Sergeant, have you had any indication from Colonel Barlow that he suspects anything is amiss here?"

"No, sir. I think the colonel believes you're at Sheridan, sir. I instructed Lieutenant Prine, as he passed through, to do nothing to destroy that notion. Prine's a good man, sir. Young, but a sincere soldier."

"Yes, I got that impression," Early said. "Very well, Sergeant. Get cleaned up and see if you can charm a meal out of Jean Stillwell." He winked. "I would suggest that you go along the creek and gather a small bouquet of flowers."

When Deeter walked away, Stella Parish said "John, I'll have to watch you. You plot too much."

"I'm sorry you said that," Early admitted. "I was going to ask you if I could ride part of the way with you." He let a smile slowly build. "After all, this is Indian country, and with two half-grown boys, a woman needs some protection."

"You could be right. All right, providing you ride all the way and stay for supper. But I might as well warn you, it's a half-day ride, and you may not find it worth it."

"I'll be getting the best of the bargain," Early said, then took the dispatch case from his belt and opened it. There was an order from Colonel Barlow for blankets, soap, candles, some cloth in bolts, and items of hardware. He frowned and said, "Would you please read this and make careful note of the items, the date, and the signature? I may need your testimony."

He saw Lieutenant Ewing on his way to the stable and whistled him over. Stella was finished, and at Early's nod she handed the dispatch to Ewing, who read it carefully, his youthful face hardening in anger.

"The sanctimonious swine," Ewing said, his voice brittle. "Shall I attend to this, sir?"

"Yes, I think you might separate the items so that Prine can load without delay. And I want each item marked and identified in some way, Mr. Ewing. Record the identifications carefully so that in the future we can positively say that this shovel or that lantern came from our supply stock. And have plenty of witnesses, Mr. Ewing."

"Yes, sir!"

"I'm going to escort Mrs. Parish and her sons home. Expect me back late tonight."

"Very good, sir."

"After dark, exercise the prisoners, one at a time, as usual. Close guard now."

"There won't be any escape, sir."

"I'm sure of that, but caution is never replaced by regret or carelessness. While the prisoners are being exercised, have your sergeant examine the cells for any attempt at escape. A man confined by himself becomes a devilish schemer, Mr. Ewing, and he'll come up with the most ingenious plans for escape."

"The cells will be searched thoroughly, sir." Ewing saluted and walked away.

Stella Parrish looked at John Early. "You're worried, aren't you?"

"Don't you think there's enough to worry about? I'm like a man bent on setting off an explosion, Stella, only my greatest concern is not dropping it before I'm ready to light the fuse." He blew out a long breath and brushed his dense moustache. "Right or wrong, win or lose, I'll be relieved of my command for this high-handed affair. But I'm willing to pay that price. It won't be just this reservation, Stella. Hell, Pine Ridge is just a patch of badlands crowded with Indians, and Earl Grover is nothing, just a little crook with a big greed. But I'll be turning a blowtorch on the whole Bureau of Indian Affairs, and every reservation will be held under a strong glass and probed and examined and culled over and curried, and when the dust settles, things will be more honest, cleaner, because a lot of people who never thought about it are going to want to know. By the same token, I know that I'm not going to improve things much. The Indian's life on reservation isn't going to turn into any pleasant, hopeful thing, but it won't be worse, and the possibility of its getting worse because of men like Grover will be lessened."

"John, Earl Grover's father is a powerful man. He's not going to stand by and see his name and his son's smeared all over the newspaper pages."

"There will be the resounding of arms," Early said wryly. "But that's an element of battle."

"You hate fighting," Stella said simply. "Is that why you fight so hard?"

He looked at her a moment, then laughed. "Call your boys and I'll take you home."

Chapter Seven

Lt. Col. George Barlow was going over the company commanders' reports when his orderly knocked and let Len Kelly, the sutler, into the office. Kelly was a small, scrawny-armed man wearing a soiled shirt and a vest with a split up the back seam.

"Hate to bother you, Colonel, but one of my teamsters came in from Hot Springs, and he told me that a load of freight went out to the reservation and not in his wagon."

Barlow's first instinct was to brush this aside as a minor irritation, but some inner caution held him from this. "Sit down, Len. Do you know this for a fact?"

Kelly shrugged. "Davis wouldn't lie to me. He's got too good a deal going with Grover." He shook his head. "Maybe you ought to ask Grover about this, Colonel. It strikes me as odd, and I wouldn't want that little runt branching out on his own. Maybe he's thinking of cutting us out."

"Don't include me!" Barlow snapped. "It's bad enough to have to sit here and watch you and Grover pocket money without being lumped in with you."

Kelly grinned. "Now, Colonel, don't take that attitude. The fact that you turn down a share don't make you less a partner. Earl and I, we think of you as one of the family."

"Get out of my office," Barlow said.

"I want you to check on Earl. He's a sneaky cuss, even if he is my cousin. But I want you to check on him, anyway. I know you'll do it after you think of it awhile. That's only fair, ain't it, Colonel? Your wife's a proud woman, good family background and all that, and she'd up and leave you if—"

"All right, all right, I'll send Grover a wire."

"Uh-uh. You ought to get on your horse and go see him."

"I can't leave my post now."

"Well, I would," Kelly said and got up and left.

George Barlow sat with his fists clenched after Kelly left, and it was several minutes before he trusted himself to move. He scooped up his kepi and went through the outer office, speaking to the clerk as he passed. "Have my horse saddled and brought to my quarters." Then he was out the door, his boots stomping the duckboards.

His wife was sitting before the front window where the morning light was good, working on some needlepoint; she looked up when he came in, surprised to see him. "Why, George, what is it?"

"I have to go to the reservation for a few days," he said. "Is there any sentiment you wish me to convey to Earl?"

"You could ask him why he doesn't write more," Harriet said. "And he never comes to the post to visit."

"I'll remind him of that," Barlow said and went into the bedroom to change into an older uniform. He took his rain cape and an extra shirt and rolled them all into a bundle; when he went to the living room, the orderly was there with his horse. "I won't be longer than I have to be," he said, kissing his wife gently.

She put her hand on his face. "George, I wish you liked Earl."

He sighed. "We can't help feeling the way we feel, Harriet. I do the best I can, don't I?"

"I'm sure you do," she said. Then she smiled. "I love you, George. You're just as dashing, as gallant today as the first time I met you."

"And you're a dear, sweet woman, Harriet." He kissed her again, more lingeringly this time, then went out and mounted his horse.

Once he'd left the post, he took the old Camp Sheridan road, figuring that he should raise the post around nine o'clock that night if he didn't dawdle, and he had no intention of doing that. Many times now he had resolved to take Earl Grover by the scruff of the neck and end this rotten affair once and for all, but he had never done it.

This time he would. It had to end. He felt that he could no longer look at Lieutenant Prine; it was difficult enough to receive Prine's report each time he went north with empty wagons and came back with them loaded heavily with goods for Kelly's shelves. The question was always in Prine's eyes, and Barlow never offered an explanation; he could only protect Prine by issuing an order in case the lieutenant was stopped or questioned. Then once the goods was on the post, the order could be torn up or burned.

When he arrived at Sheridan an alert sentry stopped him, then passed him on to headquarters, where Lieutenant Deacon came out to meet him. A trooper took the colonel's horse to the stable, and Barlow went inside with Deacon.

"Has Captain Early retired?" Barlow asked.

"The captain is at the reservation," Deacon said. "Shall I have the cook fix you something to eat, sir?"

"Thank you, yes—I haven't had a hot meal since breakfast."

Deacon went out to give his order to the sergeant of the guard, and George Barlow lit a cigar and walked up and down the office, silently cursing the luck that made Early choose this time to go to the reservation. Barlow wanted to handle this alone, for Early would make a most unsympathetic witness.

Deacon returned. "The cook will fix something for you right away. I had the sergeant light the lamp in your quarters."

"Thank you, Mr. Deacon; that was most considerate."

After he'd eaten, Barlow drew on his cigar and blew smoke toward the ceiling. "Mr. Deacon, when did Captain Early leave for the reservation?"

The notion to lie crossed Deacon's mind, but he knew Early wouldn't want him to do that. He said, "The captain has been there almost a month now, sir." He saw Barlow's head lift and the alertness come into his eyes, but he pretended not to notice or care. "The captain will be delighted to see you, sir."

"Yes, yes, I'm sure," Barlow murmured, hardly moving his lips. He hid behind a cloud of cigar smoke and walked around as though he had a restlessness that wouldn't wear off. "Of course, Captain Early has always been an officer who has taken his duties very seriously." He looked at Joe Deacon. "Perhaps too seriously, wouldn't you say?"

"I hardly see how that's possible, sir."

"What I meant was that zeal is a great thing, unless it's carried too far. We can't right the world's wrongs, Mr. Deacon. I'm sure you can see the merit of that. It's a world of give-and-take and sometimes there's more take than give—we must learn to endure unfair treatment. Some things just can't be rectified."

"Are you talking about me, Colonel, or Captain Early?"

"Perhaps both," Barlow said. "Mr. Deacon, surely you must have considered the marts of trade as being more rewarding than a military career, especially after your—unfortunate experience." He waved his hand. "And John Early surely could have been earning a handsome salary as an employee of the railroad; he has a degree in engineering and a wealth of experience. What makes a man hang on, Mr. Deacon? Answer it for yourself if you feel you can't speak for John Early."

Joe Deacon sat for a moment on the edge of the desk, a thoughtful expression on his face. Then he said, "Sir, I think it's giving in that a man hates. Especially when giving in proves someone is right when they were wrong all the time. I drove a woman to town because her husband was a fool and didn't know how to treat her. I drove her to town because she wanted to leave him. Afterward he needed something to save his pride, so he merely had to say that I made love to her behind his back, and people were ready to believe it. You believe it now, sir."

"The facts seemed apparent enough," Barlow said. "After all, a field-grade officer doesn't lie."

Joe Deacon looked at him a moment, then laughed. "Colonel, you're a very funny man. I suppose you believe in the bunny rabbit, too."

"Don't go too far with me!"

"How far is that, sir? I think I'd like to find out. John Early already knows, I think." He got off the desk and faced Barlow. "I'm a loser, Colonel, so I'll come out and say what I think. I *know* you can be bought. So it's just a matter of establishing the price, isn't it?"

Barlow looked like a man who is about to fight, then the stiffness went out of him and he half turned away and puffed his cigar. "I'm very tired, Mr. Deacon. If you'll excuse me, I'll go to my quarters."

"Very well, sir. I'll call the sergeant."

"No need for that. I'll find my way." He turned to the door, then stopped. "What's going on at the reservation?" He waited for Deacon to say something, and when he didn't, Barlow smiled. "Don't know, or won't say? Well, it doesn't matter. Good night."

There was a lamp burning in quarters farther down the walk, he went there and found an orderly waiting. They exchanged salutes, then Barlow went in and closed the door. The bed looked comfortable, and the place was clean, with a pitcher of fresh water on the pine dresser. He sat down and tugged off his boots and smoked the short cigar; then he snubbed it out, blew out the lamp, undressed, and got into bed.

He was tired and troubled, and worry was a weight he had borne so long that it crushed him without his being really aware of it. The fact that Early was at the reservation, had been at the reservation, filled Barlow with a complete dread. Regardless of Grover's confidence that John Early would cooperate, George Barlow knew better.

Early did not deal and compromise and cooperate because he didn't have to, but Barlow supposed that only another military man would know that, one who lived by position on the promotion roster and advanced from review board to review board. It would take a career man to really understand that there was nothing ahead for Early but service, no advancement or hope of it. And when a dedicated man found himself in that position, he could afford scruples that boggled the mind of the rank climber, the officer who had to play a little politics to change his gold leaf to silver, or his silver leaf to an eagle.

He slept soundly. The bugler woke him, and a moment later, while he was dressing, a sergeant knocked with Deacon's invitation to breakfast.

Thirty minutes later Barlow was mounted and riding out of Sheridan. He expected to reach the agency buildings by sundown, and as he put the post behind him, he felt certain that Lt. Joe Deacon would telegraph John Early and warn him of the arrival.

Around noon Barlow stopped for fifteen minutes, but other than that he maintained a steady march, walking his horse from time to time, but keeping at it, as though hurrying were going to do him some good. Now and then he saw smoke rising from Indian fires, and it gave him an odd feeling to be riding through their land this way and not meet trouble, but they paid no attention to him. He did not stop until he reached the main reservation buildings.

The sun was down behind a high bank of clouds, and a trooper took his horse while he beat some of the dust from his clothes. John Early came out of the main building, pausing on the porch. "Colonel, this is quite a surprise."

Barlow was in no mood for diplomacy. "Don't hand me that. Deacon wired you this morning."

Early shook his head. "Joe knows better than to send a telegram unless there's a strategic reason behind it. Your arrival, Colonel, may have been awkward, but hardly of great importance."

Color stained Barlow's cheeks, and he snapped, "I like your friendly, frank manner, John." He looked around. "Where's Earl Grover?"

"Locked up," Early told him. "George, you'd better come inside and sit down and have a drink. You're going to need it." He held open the door, shooing the flies away while Barlow stepped inside. Lieutenant Ewing was doing some paper work, and he gathered it up and left, his manner stiff and barely civil. Barlow was of a mind to say something about that, but Early kept tugging at his arm, getting him to sit down and putting a drink in front of him.

"George, I'm going to give it to you without any sugar coating: I've got nothing but bad news for you. First off, I arrested Grover and Marley as soon as I arrived here." He held up his hand when Barlow opened his mouth to dispute that. "I know, you wired Grover and he answered." He shook his head. "*I* answered, George. And I hung on to your requisition long enough to have it photographed." He reached behind him to the desk drawer and brought out the first edition of the Pine Ridge *Enterprise*, handing it to

Barlow so he could see the front page and the photographed documents. There was momentary agony in Barlow's eyes, as though he viewed an explosion that wiped out completely every effort he had ever made.

Early said, "By this time, George, this paper is in the hands of editors from Baltimore to San Francisco. You're done in, George. Finished. There's nothing you can do about it except shoot yourself, retire, or stand pat and face the court-martial." He slapped the newspaper. "I've got Grover and Marley and likely the sutler at your post and maybe the freight line that hauls the supplies here and quite probably the supply house in Council Bluffs where Grover has been ordering everything. Every document, record book, voucher, and entry has been photographed and filed. I'd like to have had another four months, but I knew it wasn't very likely. Grover's father would want to know why his son didn't write, or you'd pay me a visit and find out I had the little bastard in the pokey."

Barlow's complexion was gray, and he spoke listlessly. "John, there's no chance at striking a chord of reason here?"

"None at all, George. Grover's a thief; he's got to go. You knew about it, worked with him; you've got to go. The rotten part has to be cut out." He leaned forward and spoke confidentially. "George, let's face facts. Suppose I took all this to Laramie and laid it in General Spencer's lap. What do you think he'd do? He'd pick up the rug and shove it under because he's getting close to his second star and a controversy might upset the whole damned thing. He'd whitewash you, send Grover home, and he'd be replaced by a man who stood every chance of being as bad. So I can't deal with Spencer. I went over his head. Not to another general, but to the public. Do you know how many people are going to read that?"

Barlow shrugged. "People read a lot of things, John. I think you've overestimated the results you're going to get."

"No, I haven't," Early said. "I've exposed Earl Grover, son of Sen. Loren Grover, a thief and embezzler. Senator Grover is going to see this paper; someone will make sure of it and send him a copy, because people like to see someone else squirm. And when he sees it, he's going to fly into a rage and see the Secretary of War."

"You'll be court-martialed, John."

"Right!"

George Barlow stared at him. "That's what you want!"

"Right," Early said, smiling. "And no one's going to duck out, George, because the Senate is going to investigate this one. Grover will demand it. He has no choice at all. Absolutely none if he ever hopes to be relected. He's got to clear his son, and to do that he'll have to nail me."

"You conniving swine," Barlow said, not really angry. "You'll drag us all down with you!"

"Give me one reason for doing otherwise."

Barlow shook his head. "This will kill my wife, John. She's Earl Grover's stepsister." He glanced at Early to see whether he was surprised at this or not. "They're very fond of each other, John. I've done a lot to keep her from being hurt. I'll go a lot further."

"Hell, go," Early snapped. "Why should I care

about you, George? You've always had it good—a full belly and comfortable quarters. Go take a look around the reservation. Look at the skinny kids and the old people so thin a good wind would pick them up and blow them away." He blew out a long breath, then went to the door and yelled for Lieutenant Ewing, who came on the double. "Mr. Ewing, you will inform the sergeant of the guard that the prisoners are to be released. Provide them with horses if they want to leave, but if they start trouble, use force to subdue them."

"Yes, sir," Ewing said. Then he looked at George Barlow, and from the man's expression Ewing knew that Barlow's career was over.

After Ewing had left, Early closed the door and went back to sit on the corner of his desk; it eased his leg considerably. "You've shattered Mr. Ewing's illusions, George. Well, it won't be the last illusion he'll lose, but each one will hurt as much as the other. Compromise always takes more out of a man than he realizes."

"In spite of this tragedy you've brought down on all of us," Barlow said, "I have to admire you in a left-handed way. Even when a man is determined to go out with a roar, it takes a certain kind of nerve to carry it off."

He looked around as footsteps rattled the boards of the porch, and then the door was flung open and Earl Grover rushed in, stopped so quickly that Marley, who was following him rammed into him.

Grover's beard was thick, and his face was dirty, and his clothes held such an odor that even across the room it was too strong for Barlow's sensitive nose.

Barlow said, "John, did you have to keep them like pigs?" He started to get up, but Marley pushed Grover aside and stepped forward, his fists doubled.

"Colonel, I'm going to beat the brains out of him. Which side are you on?"

"We've all been found out," Barlow said dully. "Does that answer your question?" His glance slid to John Early. "Sorry, but I've got to get something out of this. Bolt the front door, Earl."

Grover laughed and did as he was told. Barlow quickly moved to the door connecting the kitchen and closed it, turning the key. John Early watched him do this, and there was no change in his expression at all; he deftly unbuckled his pistol belt and put it in the desk, locking the drawer and pocketing the key.

Dan Marley ripped the sleeves from his filthy shirt and threw them aside, then rolled his shoulders and shuffled forward toward Early, who seemed quite unconcerned about it all. Then Marley jumped and swung, and Early put all his weight on his good leg and slipped to one side, letting the drive of Marley's swing carry him, belly down, across the desk.

He aimed for a spot behind Marley's ear, but he missed it and caught him at the base of the neck, hurting him and carrying him on over the desk to the floor. A chair went over and broke under Marley's weight, and this noise attracted Lieutenant Ewing, who pounded on the front door and demanded to be let in.

Marley was getting up, shaking his head, leaning on the desk for support, and George Barlow said, "For God's sake, Dan, stop being so clumsy."

"I'll get him," Marley said and moved around the desk. Early came to him, met him at the corner, and was staggered by a blow to the face. He went back to keep his balance, threw all his weight on his bad leg, and it gave way with him, putting him down.

This was a chance Marley wouldn't pass up, and he aimed a kick at Early, meaning to catch him in the thigh and put his good leg out of action, but Early rolled and took it on the rump. Before Marley could kick again, Early was getting up, blood streaming down his cheek where Marley's knuckles had gashed him. Early staggered a bit, and Marley rushed in to take advantage of this. Barlow yelled but he was too late; Marley had been suckered into the trap and Early's fist was like a sledge against the bridge of his nose.

Early wasn't trying to knock him out; that would be too risky. He was cutting Marley down to size and the blow made both Marley's eyes fill with tears and blood gushed and for a moment he was blind. Early needed no more; he plunged his fist into the man's stomach, brought up his knee and caught the bent-over man flush in the face, arching him up again. Then when Early had his target, he swung and broke Marley's jaw.

The man made a complete pivot as he fell, and he skidded on his shoulder before coming against the legs of a stout table. Lieutenant Ewing was still trying to batter the door down. Early walked over and shot the bolt back; Ewing nearly fell headlong into the room.

He recovered and looked around, and Early motioned toward Marley. "Mr. Ewing, please get that man out of here." He looked at Barlow and Earl Grover. "You gentlemen will please remain." Then he walked over to Barlow and put his nose two inches from the colonel's. "Sir, if it is the last thing I ever do, I'll see you stripped of rank and honors and drummed out of the officers' corps. Have I made myself clear, George?"

"I always understood that," Barlow said. "But the opening gun has just sounded, and you're too good a soldier to know that a battle can be won on the first attack." He turned. "Come on, Earl, let's get out of here. You can file your charges at Fort Robinson." He wrinkled his nose in distaste. "God, do you need a bath!"

"I want to pack my things" Grover said. "I have a right to my personal belongings. Captain I demand that you furnish two wagons."

John Early sighed. "Mr. Ewing, if Mr. Grover is not gone in five minutes, I order you to throw him bodily off the reservation."

"My pleasure, sir," Ewing said and then dragged Dan Marley outside and rolled him off the porch. A large crowd had gathered, and Dr. Mulvahill made a brief examination but offered no advice or assistance.

When they all stepped outside, Grover saw Cal Ormond and his cowboy friends standing to one side, guarded by a handful of troopers. Grover rushed over to the man, grabbed his coat, and promptly got knocked flat. Ormond said, "You little bastard, because of you I rot in jail!" He kicked Earl Grover in the ribs and got a howl out of him.

Early said, "Sergeant, don't allow Mr. Ormond to do that. Give them their horses and firearms and see that they leave the reservation."

Then he turned and went inside and closed the door. In the washroom he looked at the cut on his face; the bleeding had stopped, so he washed it and forgot about it. He could hear what went on outside, but paid no attention to it.

As Colonel Barlow had said, the opening gun had sounded and the battle was on; the victor was yet undecided, but Early reckoned that his chances were strong. He went into the kitchen, where Jean Stillwell was peeling potatoes. Harry Kitchen's boy was perched on a stool, watching her and munching a soda cracker.

"Why didn't you come in and see the fight?" Early asked, going to the coffeepot.

"I could hear it. Besides, I knew how it would turn out."

"For a moment there I wasn't sure," Early admitted. He leaned against the sink drainboard. "I'm not sure when, but I suppose in about ten days, perhaps less, I'll be relieved of my command and charged with an impressive list of offenses. I don't know who will be in charge of the agency then, so it might be a good idea if you made plans accordingly. Who can say what will happen?"

She looked at him, then said, "What can be worse than the way it was?"

He nodded. "In a few days I want to hold another ration. Butler can pass the word around. If everyone takes enough to hold them for a while—"

"You're more concerned for them than you are for yourself," Jean Stillwell said. "John, that's not right. We need you here."

"You'll get a good man," he assured her, then drank his coffee.

As he rinsed the cup, she said, "How was your ride to Stella Parish's place?"

He smiled. "Nice."

"You're the first man I ever knew her to invite. That must mean something."

"Don't let your imagination run away with you," he suggested.

"I'm not. Just don't sell yourself short where the right woman's concerned. I thought I'd convinced you of that."

He left the kitchen and remained in his office for a time, but he began to feel restless. Finally he got his pistol belt and put it on and went to the stable for his horse. As he rode across the parade, he saw Phil Ewing and stopped. "I'm going off the reservation for a day or so. You're in command."

"Yes, sir."

"Lieutenant Kitchen should be back this afternoon. Inform him of all that's happened."

"Where will you be, sir?"

Early waved to the west. "Camped out there someplace. I may stop at Stella Parish's place." He kneed the horse into motion and rode away, wondering why he just hadn't been able to come out and tell Ewing that his destination had been the Parish place all along. And after he thought about it, he realized that he was afraid others would laugh at him for even favoring a woman. He had once found it comical to see an old man flirt with a young woman, and now others might find it humorous to see him do the same thing.

As he passed through the reservation, he drew a lot of attention and Indians came out to greet him. Among them there were some he had fought, and he had their respect and their trust because he made no promises to them that he did not keep.

He carried behind his horse a string of gay children; they followed him until they had to turn back but, others always joined the procession, and now and then he would hoist one to the saddle for a ride on his horse.

As he left the reservation, left the squalor and the hopelessness behind, it occurred to him that these people did not understand justice or peace or law; they understood hungry bellies, and if those bellies were filled, then they were ready to understand some other thing.

When he reached the Parish ranch, he lifted the horse into a trot, for he could see the house in the far distance, across the valley and backed against the foothills. Off to his right he saw two men mounted and thought they were the Parish boys; they changed direction and rode toward him, and because of that he stopped and waited for them.

It was only when they were close that he saw who the riders were, and then it was too late, for Cal Ormond whooped, drew his gun, and spurred his horse. A hundred yards separated them, and Early turned his horse, drew his long-barreled pistol and cocked it.

The rider with Ormond trailed him by ten yards, and he seemed to have no intention of catching up or passing Ormond, so Early kicked his horse into a jump just as Ormond got off his first shot. Early never knew where the bullet went; he was riding off at a tangent, making Ormond change direction.

Then Early stopped his horse, turned him, aimed and fired and watched Ormond roll from the saddle. He hit the ground and bounced, and the rider with him veered off, then stopped just out of pistol range and watched as Early rode over and dismounted.

The shooting had attracted the Parish boys, they were coming across the valley, but he paid no attention to them. He holstered his pistol and knelt and rolled Cal Ormond over. The shot had hit him high in the chest, ranged across and penetrated both lungs.

He was dead.

Early straightened and called to the man out there sitting his horse. "Come on in! No trouble unless you want it."

The man hesitated, then raised his right hand high and rode in; he arrived a moment before the Parish brothers got there. They were not accustomed to seeing dead men, and their eyes got round, and they kept swallowing hard.

John Early said, "Take him along with you, mister. Tell the sheriff how it happened. You know where to find me."

"Will you help me load him?" the cowboy asked. When Early nodded, he caught up Ormond's horse and they lifted the man across the saddle. The cowboy tied him on and said, "Cal was always a damned fool. It was just a matter of time before someone stopped him. But I don't guess his wife'll understand that."

The cowboy mounted up, took the reins, and slowly rode in the direction he had come. The Parish boys watched John Early; there was a grimness in his face that held them silent, and it was only after he was mounted again and turning toward the house that he spoke. "You've seen a man throw himself away because he was proud."

Ken, the older boy, said, "I guess he shot first."

Early looked at him a moment. "Does that really matter now?"

"I guess it don't," the boy admitted.

"The less we say of this to your mother," Early said, "the better it will be. Understand?"

They nodded solemnly. "Ma heard the shooting," Bill said. "She'll want to know."

"Then I'll explain it," Early said. "You must trust my judgment in these matters, boys."

"We do," Ken said.

Stella Parish was waiting for them as they rode into the yard; the boys went on to the barn and the chores there, and Early tied his horse in the shade. She came up to him. "I heard the shooting. Was that Cal Ormond?"

"Yes. He felt that he had something that just had to be settled." He walked to the well for a cool drink of water, and she followed him and worked the windlass for him. "It was settled. As finally as anything can be settled, much to my regret."

"I saw you and the other man draping him across his horse," Stella said. "John, don't be a fool now and blame yourself for anything. I'm sure he fired first."

He looked at her. "Your son said that. Why are you so sure I was fair with him? Don't you think I can make mistakes?" He caught up his temper and blew out his breath. "There, I almost made one. I almost blamed you for the fact that I feel rotten and have come to the end of my rope and know now that I'm sorry, that I care more than I thought I did."

She took his arm. "Come on into the house. I'm glad you came here."

"I really don't have a good reason," he said.

"Don't you?"

"Well, I came because I needed someone."

Her smile was a quick, bright thing. "Why, that's the best reason of all."

She made him sit at the kitchen table and gave him a piece of peach pie and a cup of coffee. A pot of stew was bubbling on the back of the stove, filling the kitchen with delicious smells. The boys were arguing by the barn, and he found the whole thing most relaxing.

"I don't want to presume on such a short acquaintance Early said. "Stella, it's too easy to be involved with other people's troubles, and I can assure you you wouldn't want mine."

"Don't be so sure all the time," she cautioned. Then she brought her coffee to the table and sat across from him. "The other night, when you sat at my table, I had the strangest feeling. No other man except my husband ever sat there, and I felt funny because I'd always sworn to myself that only he had the right, and at the time I wasn't feeling guilty at all. And I couldn't tell you that even though I wanted to."

"But you're telling me now."

"You came here—that's reaching for me. I'm only reaching, too, John."

He smiled. "I'd like to believe that."

"Then believe it." She studied his face, his mood carefully. "I'm like you—I want to reach out while there's still time. No one likes loneliness, but there are people like you and me who just won't accept substitutes." She took his hand and held it. "Promise me something? If you feel anything for me, don't hold it back. No matter what reason you may think you have, don't hold it back."

He looked at her, then smiled and spoke softly. "Why do you think I've come back so soon?"

Chapter Eight

Gen. Harvard Calhoun was having dinner with his wife and family when the servant came in and announced that Sen. Paul Augusta and party were waiting in the library on an urgent matter. This annoyed Calhoun, but he was too old a hand at politics to let any of it show; he politely excused himself and left the dining room, walking down the length of the entrance hall to the library, which was just to the left of the front entrance.

Senator Augusta and his friends were already thickening the air with their cigars; they got up as Calhoun entered, and they shook hands. Augusta was a very small man, dark, with Spanish blood running back many years before California became the domain of the American. "I'm sorry to interrupt your dinner, General," he said. "You know Senator Burger and Senator Estes."

There was an exchange of pleasantries, then Augusta pulled the evening edition of the *Post* out of his coat pocket. "Have you seen this, General?"

"No. I read after dinner," Calhoun said.

"Well, you'd better read this," Estes said. He was a florid man with a reputation for fearless debate and a voice that could easily drown out the opposition. "And you'd better sit down to do it."

Calhoun took the paper and started to read, ignoring Estes's advice, but he had barely read the headlines before he fumbled for the arm of his chair and finished the article sitting down. It ran to the inside pages, and when Calhoun had finished, he left the paper in his lap.

Paul Augusta said, "General, are you acquainted with Captain Early? I ask that in order to establish the reputation of the man. Is this article factual, sound?"

"I know Captain Early well," Calhoun said. "I would stake my reputation on the exactitude of it."

Augusta looked at the others and blew out a long breath. "That's what we wanted to know, General. As you may know, we have neither love nor respect for Senator Grover, and there's going to be one hell of a stink over this. We've been at a meeting with the Secretary of War, and Grover is demanding a full investigation and the immediate court-martial of Captain Early."

"Naturally," Calhoun said, "but of course Early expects that. It may be just what he wants."

Sen Orin Burger, a slender down-Easter with a twang in his voice, said, "General, we've convinced the Secretary that an investigation should be held immediately, if for no other reason that to satisfy the newspapers. Senator Augusta has been appointed to that committee, and Senator Grover. I'm on it, and Senator Estes. The large portion of the meeting was devoted to who would chair the committee, as it is almost impossible to select a man who has no political ax to grind. It was agreed that you would be a splendid choice, General. Will you do it?"

Calhoun frowned. "Gentlemen, this is most unusual."

"Yes, we readily admit that, but time is of the essence here. Certainly an investigation is called for, in light of the seriousness of the whole thing and the repercussions it is bound to have. The military is deeply involved, General. The large question that will have to be settled, before any specific charges can be made, is whether or not Captain Early had the right to take over the function of an Indian reservation, regardless of the circumstances." He shook his head. "There are many facets to this, General, and it's going to be a long time before we get to the bottom of it. Will you accept the chairmanship?"

"Yes," Calhoun said.

Ronald Estes said, "General, I suggested that the committee meet in ten days at Fort Laramie. This will give the principals an opportunity to assemble, and those reluctant will be brought there by U. S. marshals. We can wire General Spencer, and he can make all the arrangements. Naturally, the press will be represented by the hundreds." He sighed, and forced a smile. "These things happen, and I can never make up my mind whether I'm happy or sorry. Some heads are liable to drop, General. Army heads as well as civilian."

Calhoun nodded. "I'm sure Captain Early knew that."

Paul Augusta laughed. "Well, he certainly picked a weapon: public opinion. I've received telegrams from my constituents who have never seen an Indian. The religious orders are up in arms; they have always felt that they've been ousted and that the only way to handle Indians is through conversion." He threw up his hands and let them drop limply. "Who is right?

Does anyone know?" Then he picked up his hat and cane. "We've disrupted your dinner too much already, General. Thank you. I know we will succeed."

A servant showed them out, and Harvard Calhoun went back to his dinner. His son, who had a successful medical practice in Baltimore, said, "You know, I vote for them, but when I think about it, I'm suspicious of all men in power—present company excepted." He let his smile fade. "I—ah—happened to read the *Post* before leaving the station. Is it—"

"Yes," Calhoun said. He glanced at his wife. "I'm sorry, my dear, but that summer in Rhode Island is going to have to be postponed. I'll be leaving for Fort Laramie in a few days. For the summer, more than likely."

Calhoun's two daughters, both at an age when selfishness and the pursuit of pleasure outweigh all else, pouted and registered their protest, but a glance from him held it from going further. "Ethel, do you remember Captain Early? A very tall man with one eye and—"

"Of course, Harvard. A most polite man and quite a hero, I understand."

"Well, he's kicked over the beehive this time," Calhoun said. "He ousted Senator Grover's son from the Pine Ridge Agency, kept him under lock and key for well over a month, and uncovered a pile of fingers-in-the-till dirt that just won't blow away."

Elliot Calhoun wiped his mouth and put the napkin aside. "Really, Father, can Captain Early hope to substantiate these charges? They're very serious and certainly will reflect on the Senator and his campaign for reelection."

"My boy, I've known John Early for many years, and never, not once, have I known him to run a bluff he couldn't back to the hilt and then some. In that man's military background there are a lot of dead Indian leaders who thought he was running a bluff on them. He's a rough tactician, but he gets results. Early takes chances no other man would accept."

"Why?" Elliot asked.

"Because he's born to lose," Harvard Calhoun said simply. "His career comes to an end each time the retirement board meets, and he knows it, dies a little, and then gets a reprieve, but he knows it can't last forever." He sighed and pushed his plate away, his appetite gone. "This time he's come to the end, and he knows it. No matter how it turns out, John Early's leaving the service will be a condition of agreement. And I think it's just too damned bad."

Chapter Nine

The sheriff had no reason to charge or hold John Early for the shooting of Cal Ormond, and he sent his deputy to Camp Sheridan to inform Early of this and take his deposition for the inquest. From the deputy's manner, Early surmised that the law-enforcement elements were relieved to be rid of Ormond, but he said nothing about this. He wrote out the deposition, had it witnessed, gave it to the deputy, then watched the man ride away.

It was, he thought, a very casual way to write the last word on a man's life, and he would never become accustomed to it. In the span of his own warring years he had quietly buried many a trooper beside an unmarked trail, and it had always bothered him— that a man would give so much and yet be denied the honor of thoughtful regret at his passing.

Early's own affairs were drawing to a close, and he quietly made his preparations, gathering together all the papers he would need to defend himself, making certain that the Indians would get their food ration, and all the time hoping that the man who would relieve him would have a little compassion toward a people who generally were considered to deserve it the least.

The telegram came from General Spencer's headquarters, relieving John Early of his command and appointing Lieutenant Phil Ewing in his place. It was a windfall that Early had not counted on, for Kitchen had not been relieved and Ewing was a sincere young man who would do the right thing.

Early sent the sergeant to find Ewing, and a few minutes later he came in. Early showed him the telegram. "I'm turning the command over to you, Mr. Ewing, with the knowledge that it is in capable hands. Please wire Lieutenant Deacon at Camp Sheridan. He undoubtedly picked it up when the message went through his operator, but to keep it official—"

"Yes, of course, sir. Captain, I'm very sorry."

"I'm not," Early said. "Phil, every man has to bow out sometime, and very few get a chance to do it with a roar." He smiled and offered his hand. "Good-bye. Good luck with your new command."

"Sir, I have a request. If they—charge you, sir, would you accept me as your counsel?"

Early frowned. "Phil, you may not realize this, but under the circumstances you could be tarred with the same brush."

"I'm aware of that, sir. I still want to act as counsel."

"Then I accept," Early said. "Good-bye. I think it's useless for me to dawdle here, so I'll catch up my horse, load my gear, and head back." He smiled. "I'm sure General Spencer has many things he wants to say to me, and none of them complimentary."

Early had a sergeant catch up his horse, and another loaded the pack horse, and Early mounted and quit the reservation, but took a slightly out-of-the way jog to Stella Parish's place. He told her that he had been relieved of his command, that his destination was Laramie and his future highly uncertain. And he suggested that it might be some time before he got to see her again.

He stayed for an early supper, then left because there was a fight waiting at Laramie and he felt the urge to get on with it, and she seemed to understand this. The boys were here and kept him from venturing a good-bye with any openly romantic overtones, yet he supposed this was just as well because his future was too uncertain to base any promises on.

Still, it disappointed him, for he knew that he was in love with this woman and that she had an affection for him of still undefined depth. Perhaps he'd never have a chance to find out, and that was a shame, for he'd lived a monastic military life, and now that it was drawing to a close, he knew what he had missed.

When he was a mile from her place, he stopped because he heard a horse coming up behind him, and he turned as she rode up and stopped. "John, you didn't really think I'd let you go without your kissing me, did you?"

"Well, the boys—"

"The boys have been sent on chores in the west pasture," Stella said, then raised herself in the stirrups, took his face in her hands, and kissed him gently. When she drew back, she was smiling. "John, you just can't come into my life and ride out again without—well, without making a few promises. I've got to have something to go on."

"The uncertainties of—"

"Uncertainties I know all about," she said. "That won't do, John. Not at all. It's not a good reason."

He smiled. "Stella, it's ridiculous, a man of my age falling in love. It's even more ridiculous to presume that you—"

"If you say that I'll hit you right in the mouth!" she snapped. "I have a right to decide for myself, and don't you dare take it away from me." She had no anger, but she wanted him to understand once and for all and never speak of it again. "If I get too lonesome—which I'm liable to—I'll come to Laramie to see you. No matter how it comes out, we'll be together. I've decided that." A smile lifted the ends of her lips. "You're what I want, John. You're just going to have to marry me—I don't see any other answer." Then she turned her horse and waved and rode back, and he sat there a moment wondering why the most dreaded hurdle in his life had really been no hurdle at all.

Fifteen minutes after he'd reached the post, and before he'd had time to bathe, shave, or change into a decent uniform, John Early was summoned to Gen. Adam Spencer's office. The general was waiting, entrenched behind his desk, with a fine head of anger worked up.

The orderly closed the door behind Early, who saluted and had it returned in a most casual manner. Spencer said, "So you're the most notorious Capt. John Early. I rather expected you to enter with a swirl of brimstone." He laughed with no humor at all. "And, my friend, you will become very familiar with brimstone before I'm through with you." He stared at Early a moment. "Damn it, you're not a bit sorry for the mess you've kicked up, are you?"

"No, General, I'm not."

"Let me tell you something, Captain: you are not going to smear me, cause talk about me, or have reflections cast on my ability."

"No, sir, I'm sure I'm not, General. I was quite content with the general's reputation when I accepted the assignment. And it should be obvious, sir, that no reflection was cast on your reputation by the articles published in the agency paper. These conditions existed before you assumed your command, and you had no way of knowing of them. I'm certain that had the general discovered these frauds he would have taken immediate and severe action." He smiled pleasantly. "That is why the general sees the foolishness of having me court-martialed now."

"I see nothing of the sort!" He snatched up some papers and waved them. "Captain, I have charges ready for my signature."

"That would be foolish, sir," Early pointed out. "I've made no point, sir, about Colonel Barlow's inspecting in the general's name. Surely an alert officer would have made a trip to the reservation since Camp Sheridan is only a support base for troops policing the agency. And that was our function, sir, to *police* the agency." He shrugged. "Of course, you and I know that the general would not soil his hands, but to others, who may have suspicions, it does look bad, sir—your allowing Colonel Barlow to act for you."

Adam Spencer leaned back in his chair, his lips pursed, his eyes pulled into narrow, wrinkled slits. "Early, you're a damned clever man. It's my own mistake that I marked you down as simply rash. But your point has merit, at that. General Calhoun might—and I say *might*, again—just might read the wrong thing into that simple, openhanded gesture of consideration for Colonel Barlow. And I'm not sure I want to go to the trouble of explaining it."

"If it can be explained satisfactorily, sir," Early pointed out. "Oh, there would be no reprimand, to be sure, but they would remember this moment of indiscretion, General. And I do believe it's your first—or the first one that ever caught up with you." Spencer surged upward out of his chair, then slowly sat down again.

He tore up the charges he had prepared, then said, "Early, I'm going to see that you're through with the army. That's a promise."

"Why, of course, General. I'm quite ready now to leave the service. Of course, I would stay on if I could, but a man should know what the end of his rope looks like." He smiled pleasantly again. "I wonder what George Barlow will do, General. He was never a man who enjoyed alternatives."

"I've relieved him of his command," Spencer said bitterly. "He'll be arriving in a day or two. Guilty or not, you've put a mark on him that will deny him any chance of further promotion."

"He shouldn't be promoted," Early said. "General, being frozen in grade isn't so bad—once you get used to it. It also has certain advantages because it gives you more latitude to do the right thing without worrying about what it'll do to your career."

Spencer frowned. "I've had to detain Earl Grover and hold him here on his own recognizance. Dan

Marley also. Now that's a Senator's son, Captain, and I've arrested him, because you left me no choice. If you're wrong—" He shook his head and blew out his breath. "Warrants have been issued for Len Kelly, the sutler, and Orin Davis, who runs the freight line. The Senate committee will be arriving in a few days, along with a horde of newspaper people. I warn you to make no statements."

"Now, General, you know that's not a proper order," Early said evenly. "As a principal in this matter, I have a right to make a statement if I see fit. Will there be anything else, General?"

"No," Spencer said. "You may go." Then as Early turned, he said, "Just a moment, Captain." He got up and came around the desk. "Tell me something honestly. Did Simmons and Calhoun give you Camp Sheridan knowing that you'd kick over the whole thing?"

"General, I think they gave me the job because they thought I'd do my duty in a military manner."

"Indeed? It seems to me that your ambition is to drag down with you as many superior officers as you can."

"Only those who deserve it, sir," Early said, then nodded politely and stepped outside.

Even the hot breath of a summer breeze felt cool to him, and he realized that Spencer was feeling the pinch badly. As commanding general of the agency police troops, he was directly responsible whether he had knowledge of irregularities or not. And Adam Spencer was worried now because conditions at Standing Rock and the Crow and Pawnee reservations could be worse than they were at Pine Ridge, and all of it was going to be found out.

And it just might terminate his career, not in disgrace, but certainly by forcing his retirement. His position, his service, was largely political, and a stain on his reputation, his record, could finish him.

As Early walked to his quarters, he wondered if Calhoun and Simmons had planned to bag Adam Spencer by implication. It was a large question, for both Calhoun and Simmons knew that John Early was a campaigner, and his command at Sheridan would certainly result in changes being made.

It was, Early decided, hard to tell about generals, because they lived in a different world and considered problems at length that no colonel knew existed.

He found the officer of the day and was assigned quarters—two comfortable rooms with a writing desk and three chairs and a washstand with an Italian marble top. A striker brought his things, and Early spent more than an hour putting them away; then he bathed and shaved and changed into a clean uniform and went to early mess.

The officers ate at separate tables, four to a table, and Early took one by himself, understanding fully that every officer on the post knew his exact status and might not want to involve himself by association.

There were half a dozen officers already eating when he sat down and double that when his meal was brought to him. They pointedly ignored him, and this amused him because there were four captains there he could call by name, having either served with them or known them well by reputation.

That he made them uncomfortable John Early understood, but then he had been making men uncomfortable for nearly fourteen years now, and he had rather settled down to the role. Finally, as he was finishing his roast beef, a captain scraped back his chair and walked over.

"Captain Early, may I introduce myself? I'm Captain Dundee." He held up his hand. "An invitation to sit is unnecessary, sir."

Early smiled. "I see. You have come over, at the request of your less stalwart friends, to tell me that you find my presence annoying. Correct?"

"Exactly."

"Then I suggest most seriously that you and your friends go to hell!"

Color vaulted into Dundee's lean face. "Sir, such a remark is uncalled for and unbecoming to a—"

"Oh, come off it!" Early snapped. "What the hell do you think you're about to do, anyway? Challenge me to meet you behind the rifle butts? Brawling could cost you your commission, and you know it. Now go and sit down and eat your custard like a good boy before you make a hopeless ass of yourself."

There was no sound made in the mess; the cooks halted work in the kitchen, and the dishwashers were still. A major and two captains, entering, paused, half in, half out. Captain Dundee stood there, his face stained by his temper and the knowledge that he had moved into an area from which there was no face-saving retreat.

Early said, "You're a young man, but surely you can see that your friends have convinced you to do something they wouldn't do themselves." He waved his hand. "Look around, Captain. Major Dandridge is smiling. What is he smiling about, Captain? And Captain Ellis seems amused." John Early looked around the room and then leaned back in his chair and smiled.

Then one of the other officers spoke to Dundee. "Burt, come on back and sit down."

John Early moved back a chair at his table and said, "Captain, won't you join me? Soldier, bring the captain's dessert over here." Dundee hesitated, then laughed softly and sat down, and instantly the room again was full of the buzz of talk and the rattle of tinware in the kitchen. The officers who had been statues at the door came in and sat down, and the table waiter brought Captain Dundee's dessert.

"I guess I'll never learn not to listen to bad advice," Dundee said. "Every time I've cut myself it's been while grinding someone else's ax."

"This cost you a couple of friends, sitting here," Early said mildly. "But then a man is forced to consider the value of friends who talk him into something they're too smart to try themselves. Surely you're not going to tell me they didn't understand that you'd be up before the post commander for starting a row."

"No, they know that, and so do I," Dundee said. "Tell me something, Captain—has anyone ever put salt on your tail? They call you the iron man. And I guess a few hate you for it."

Early arched an eyebrow, saying, "And they almost convinced you that you did?"

Burt Dundee was a perceptive man; he thought

for a moment, then said, "No, that's not it. But they did arouse in me feelings of inadequacy. You might say that there I was, and there you sat, and I had to face the fact that you were as good as I was and you only had one—"

He cut it off quickly, as though afraid he was being indelicate.

Early said, "—one arm and one eye? I've also got a gimped leg that bothers me a great deal." He laughed softly. "Eat your dessert, Captain. Argument upsets the digestion."

Gen. Harvard Calhoun arrived, and everyone knew it, for there was a parade inspection and the bugler blew "The General," and after the ruffles and flourishes were done with, Calhoun was settled in Quarters. It seemed that he had hardly changed his uniform before he broke an old established custom and failed to invite the commanding officer to call.

Instead, he sent for Capt. John Early, and that raised a storm of talk around the post and made the commanding officer mad as hell.

Calhoun had the drinks poured, and he dismissed the enlisted man who was the striker for Quarters A, then waved Early into a comfortable chair. "John, for as long as I've known you, you've exceeded my fondest expectations." He raised his glass in salute. "My compliments, and if I can, I'll get you out with a whole skin."

"That's very kind of you, General, but I'm afraid you leave me more puzzled than reassured."

"We'll see if we can't straighten that out," Calhoun said, sitting down across from Early. "I won't insult you by asking how true are the charges you flung at all and sundry; I have assumed they are true. As a matter of fact, you have really charged no one, but the presentation of facts in that damned little newspaper will bring down charges." He leaned forward. "Did Colonel Barlow actually engage in the transfer of supplies as reported?"

"Yes, sir. It turns out that Mrs. Barlow is Earl Grover's stepsister, and Barlow went along with it to protect her family name."

Calhoun snorted through his nose. "To hell with the family name! I'm going to chair the investigating committee. Senator Grover will be on it, but there are three other Senators on it, too, who have it in for him. It's going to be a very warm summer in Laramie, John. There'll be deals made, and you don't like deals, but this is high politics and we've got to do the best we can for the most people involved. Sen. Loren Grover will want to protect his own name first and his son second. I'm certain that he won't be able to whitewash his son, but he might offer a deal that will keep him out of prison. We'll want to listen carefully to his offer, John."

"Dealing with that kind of man doesn't appeal to me, sir."

"To hell with you," Calhoun said bluntly. "John, I'd throw you away if that were what it took to get the job done. Senator Grover is a powerful man, and a deal with him may get us the very things we want, the very things you were ordered to do." He nodded. "When there's something rotten around, sooner or later someone with a sensitive nose is going to smell it. The Indians didn't take this lying down, John. I got a letter six months ago from a girl at Pine Ridge. Her name was—ah—Caswell? No, Stillwell. Jean Stillwell. She laid it right out in black and white, saying that Earl Grover was stealing from the Indians by selling supplies to the army post at Robinson and to ranchers. She explained how Grover 'bought' beef." He shrugged his heavy shoulders. "Now just what could I do? Take it to the Bureau of Indian Affairs? They'd have claimed she was a crank, a troublemaker, written to Grover, and he'd have been warned in time to pull in his horns. Or if he thought the game was worth it, he might have had her killed. And suppose I had sent a good, competent officer in there to look into it. Do you think he would have taken the risks you've opened yourself up for?" Calhoun shook his head violently. "John, I needed a man who would charge hell with a canteen of water and figure he had nothing to lose."

"I see," Early said. "And Kitchen, Deacon, and Murray Butler were—"

"—were good men in the same boat," Calhoun finished for him. "John, hate me for this if you want to. Cuss me if you want—it's off the record, but I'll promise you this: if we get out of this with our skins intact, I'll skip you up the promotion list if I have to address Congress myself."

"General, I didn't act out of selfish—"

Calhoun waved him silent. "Hell, I know that, but when the smoke's cleared, we're going to have to put in a man who can clean up the thing so that this doesn't happen again. You can be sick and get well and get sick again from the same thing, you know." He brought out his cigar case and offered one and a light. "I want to talk to you about this hearing, John. It is not a trial. The individual Senators are free to ask questions, as I will be, and each will be represented by the best counsel money can buy. They'll dig and probe and cut into you and everyone else until the blood runs, and the rules of hearsay evidence will not hold too well, as they would in court."

He paused to pour another drink. "Grover's chance, and, I figure, his only chance, will be to undercut the witnesses against his son to the extent that their reliability will be questioned and even doubted. I don't think, with the physical evidence that you've accumulated, he has a chance of getting his son off clean, but he can tone it down to the point where he can offer a deal. I want you to be prepared, John, because they'll turn a blowtorch on you when they start questioning you. I'd be certain I had a competent man representing me."

"I've agreed to accept Lieutenant Ewing, sir."

"Never heard of him. An attorney?"

"No, sir. A quartermaster officer."

"Good God!" Calhoun said and closed his eyes. "I happen to know that Grover is bringing one of the sharpest trial laywers in New York."

"I hope the summer weather doesn't bother him, sir."

"That's right, you be casual about it," Calhoun pointed out. "But you'll change your mind, and I hope before it's too late. You can call what witnesses you need, John. Federal marshals will be available to serve the papers and bring any of those who exhibit reluctance."

Early said, "Sir, who is your counsel?"

"You," Calhoun said flatly. "And don't say anything; I know what I'm doing. That's why I have two stars on my shoulder boards." He took his cigar out of his mouth and leaned forward. "A little deception never hurt a commander, especially when he was trying to surround a pretty smart enemy like Loren Grover. It's no problem to know who will be testifying on any following day, and we can meet quietly someplace and talk it over so that I can ask the right questions and know what is the truth and what isn't. Grover will likely think I'm an egotist who considers himself too damned smart to have counsel, and he may be lulled into making a mistake."

"That sounds logical, sir. But I'd have to know the Senator to say," Early admitted. He puffed on his cigar for a moment, then asked, "General, if this isn't a trial, what is the ultimate aim?"

"First, to establish the truth of conditions at the agency. This will determine largely the course of action the committee takes. If they find conditions as portrayed in your nespaper, they'll more than likely recommend that the responsible parties—meaning Earl Grover and ilk—be bound over in custody of the marshals and charged formally. Then, of course, there would be a trial." He hunched down in his chair. "And that's the moment when Sen. Loren Grover is going to offer his deal to us. And we'll neither reject it nor jump at it. Instead we'll consider it, and if it does the job we want, we'll accept it."

"I hate that idea, sir."

Calhoun laughed. "John, be a realist. The day of total defeat is long gone. You get part of what you want with the surrender terms, and you learn to live with it."

Chapter Ten

The post commander, a colonel within a year of retirement age and fervently hoping it would be quiet and uneventful, had his post turned into a carnival, with more civilians billeted there than officers. This required a good deal of doubling up, especially in the junior grades, and mumbling went on constantly about having to give up a room so that "those damned newspaper people can cut us to pieces."

The junior officers' grumbling was nothing compared to that of the captains and two majors who had to move out of their quarters to make room for the Senators and their retinue. The two majors were married and gave up their houses so that Sen. Loren Grover and his following could move in. Immediately Grover applied pressure on the post commander, and Colonel Barlow and his wife moved in so that she could be near her stepfather.

General Calhoun invited Senators Burger and Estes to stay at Quarters A; they accepted, and Senator Augusta took a hotel room in town, although it meant a four-mile ride each way morning and night.

Post routine was difficult under the weight of all these people, and the newspapermen were everywhere, trying to interview, question, talk, probe—anything to get something for the paper paying their expenses.

The post telegraph was sorely taxed, and the quartermaster officer, charged with feeding and housing these people, saw his budget knocked hopelessly out of kilter, and he had to appeal to the commanding officer for emergency funds just to replenish his stores.

Captain Early was invited to Quarters A to meet Orin Burger and Ronald Estes, and Paul Augusta delayed his evening trip to town in order to accept General Calhoun's invitation. And because it had to be done, Calhoun included Senator Grover, who arrived twenty minutes late.

He was a surprise to John Early; although he was short, like his son, Grover had a pinched, ferocious expression and large brooding eyes, and as soon as he handed his hat and cane to the orderly, he stepped into the room as though he had come to give them all orders.

Calhoun said, "Senator, may I present Capt. John Early."

Grover looked up at Early, who extended his hand; then he slapped Early across the face, throwing all his strength into it. Early staggered sideways a step, and blood rushed to the imprint of Grover's hand.

Then Early said, "As I always believed, we in the military can learn so much in the way of manners from a gentleman."

Senator Estes tried not to, but he couldn't help laughing, and General Calhoun stood there, rocking back and forth on his heels, so proud he didn't know what to do about it.

Grover's scowl deepened, and he took on deep color, as a man will when he's made an irreparable error in judgment. He let his anger tow him along. "Captain, right to your face I'll call you an unmitigated liar and a scoundrel!"

"My apologies," Early said, "for I don't know you well enough to properly label *you*, Senator. A condition, however, that will soon be corrected."

Paul Augusta said, "Well, Senator, now that you've let us all see the more charming side of your personality, shall we go into the dining room? The general has been kind enough to hold off dinner until you arrived." He chuckled softly. "One of these days you ought to buy a watch."

"You didn't think I'd come," Loren Grover snapped. "That's what you thought. Well, I'm no coward, sir!" He spun around and faced John Early. "And you've misread my son badly, sir. That's a mistake that will cost you dearly."

Orin Burger stepped up and took Grover by the arm. "Come on in to dinner, Loren. One thing about you that's outstanding is that you get very tiresome quickly."

They sat down around the table, Harvard Calhoun at the end and John Early on his left. The meal was served immediately, for the cook had been keeping the mashed potatoes hot without drying them out, and another ten minutes would have made this impossible.

Ronald Estes made an honest and partially successful effort to get small talk going, but he couldn't keep the conversation steered into clear channels.

Finally Loren Grover said, "I would like to caution each of you until the full facts are known." He smiled.

"And you will find them quite different from the allegations made by Captain Early in his cheap yellow rag."

"I think there is no danger in that," General Calhoun said. "There is no need to delay, so I believe we can call the committee to order at ten o'clock tomorrow morning."

Grover frowned. "General, it is unreasonable to begin so quickly. A few days or a week is a reasonable delay."

"There's no reason for it," Calhoun said. "Captain Early is ready to testify, and he claims to have his witnesses available." He looked around the table. "Gentlemen, I think ten o'clock tomorrow is reasonable. Agreed?" Grover shook his head, but he was the only one, and the matter was settled.

"My son is willing to testify," Loren Grover maintained. "And since he has been most cruelly wronged, I think it only proper that he be given a chance to tell his side of this distorted affair."

Senator Burger said, "Loren, your son has been accused. In essence he is defending himself. Therefore the state, so to speak, should present its case and rest on it."

"This is not a trial," Grover insisted.

"True, but it should follow logical rules of order," Burger said. "Do you agree, General?"

Calhoun pursed his lips a moment. "Frankly, I don't see the difference in who starts first. We're after facts, the truth. It isn't a matter of proving Earl Grover guilty or Captain Early a liar." He looked at Early. "Are you ready to present your arguments and rest it there?"

"Yes," Early said.

Ronald Estes said, "I should warn you, sir, that you will be attacked bitterly and will not have a chance to question witnesses until Earl Grover testifies. The newspaper people may take, advantage of this for the sake of copy and paint you quite black."

John Early looked squarely at Loren Grover and laughed. "Gentlemen, considering the color I'm going to splash on the Senator's son, any shade the newspapermen daub on me is bound to look like sunrise in comparison. Let's get the music started because I'm a dancing man."

There was a moment of silence around the table, then General Calhoun said, "Well, I think that pretty well sets the tenor of things. There's no need in pretending that we're all friends. Before this is over, some of us here are going to get pretty badly clawed. One or two may not survive it. Senator Grover, you'll be fighting for your political life, as well as the freedom of your son." He looked at Orin Burger and Paul Augusta. "For fifteen years you've been trying to sink a hook into Senator Grover. You've fought him on the floor and in the newspapers. If there's a word that can be called dirty and still be repeated in mixed company, then you've called each other that. For spite and revenge you've blocked legislation that would have done a lot of people a lot of good. I would say, gentlemen, that service on this committee, if the results do not embrace correct action, could cost you a lot of power, and perhaps reelection."

"What about you, General?" Estes asked wryly.

"I haven't forgotten myself," Calhoun admitted. "I've backed Captain Early for a number of years, and if I've been wrong, if he's been wrong, then this general is going to be automatically retired from the service. So we all have a lot to lose and not a great deal to gain. But we're going to start at ten o'clock tomorrow morning, anyway."

"Succinctly put," Augusta said. "Now I'm ready for my coffee and cigar." He smiled and pushed back his chair.

Gen. Harvard Calhoun called the committee to order at the appointed hour. The main pavilion of the Fort Laramie officers' club was crowded to capacity with newspapermen and photographers representing every major magazine and periodical. General Calhoun opened the hearing by explaining that they were authorized by the Secretary of War and that testimony would be taken down and made part of the record in the form of a report. Witnesses would testify under oath administered by a U. S. marshal appointed by the committee, and the committee members were free to question witnesses and recall them for reexamination.

With the ground rules established, General Calhoun said, "The committee will call Capt. John Early, United States Cavalry."

The marshal repeated the call, although it was not necessary, for Early was already walking forward. He raised his hand, repeated the oath, and sat down.

"State your full name, please," Calhoun said.

"John Charles Early."

"I have here a copy of a four-page newspaper, the Pine Ridge *Enterprise*. In it you have made some very serious charges against employees of the United

States Government, and an officer in the United States Army. Are you prepared to swear to the validity of these charges?"

"I am, sir." Early shifted in the chair and crossed his legs. "Gentlemen, I can save the committee a great deal of time by presenting reliable witnesses who will swear under oath that these irregularities took place. Lieutenant Prine, Quartermaster Department, has, upon numerous occasions and under direct orders from Col. George Barlow, received stores and supplies from the Pine Ridge Agency, transported them to Fort Robinson, and deposited them in the sutler's warehouse. These stores and supplies, bought with government funds and intended for the health and welfare of the Indians, were then sold and the profit divided by prearranged agreement."

Orin Burger said, "Just a minute, Captain. You say the stores and supplies were sold at Fort Robinson. Can you prove that?"

"I cannot swear to direct knowledge of the sale, sir, but I am convinced that investigation will prove it for me. If the supplies were not sold or disposed of, then they should still be in inventory at Fort Robinson."

Loren Grover had a question. "Captain, what proof do you have that these supplies were transported or disposed of illegally?"

"As to exact knowledge that the sutler sold them, I have already answered that I couldn't swear to this. However, I am prepared to prove that additional supplies and stores were sold directly to ranchers in the vicinity of the reservation. I can produce names, dates, sworn testimony as to the transactions and that the money, in cash, was handed over to Earl Grover or his assistant, Dan Marley. Supplies and stores were also sold to the merchants in Hot Springs, and they will so swear. These transactions were in cash, and the goods was transported by Orin Davis's freight line. He is presently in custody and is ready to swear to his part of the business." He raised a finger. "Lieutenant Prine's testimony links Colonel Barlow with the agent, Earl Grover, and deeply implicates the sutler. Orin Davis, who hauled goods for the agent, is willing to tell everything in order to limit the criminal charges that threaten him." He held up the third finger. "I can produce witnesses who will testify that the Indians were sick and starving. Witnesses who will testify that Earl Grover used Indian labor to provide a luxurious mode of living and paid them off in food, which they were entitled to in the first place." He made his fourth point. "I have witnesses who will testify that Earl Grover signed receipts for beef that was never delivered, paid half the stipulated price to the cattleman, and put the other half in his own pocket." He slapped the arm of his chair. "You gentlemen want witnesses? I have witnesses, one after the other: Dr. Mulvahill at the agency, Stella Parish from the T Bar Ranch, sergeants, corporals—if you want witnesses, I have them."

"There are witnesses, and then there are witnesses," Loren Grover said, smiling. "Captain, let me ask you some personal questions. Isn't it a fact that for some years now you have remained in the service largely through inaction of the retirement board?"

Early took his time; he wasn't going to be stampeded by Grover, who was loading his questions to maim. "You might say that, sir, if you say it in the same sense that you have remained in office simply because the voters have not risen in a body and demanded your recall."

This raised a gale of laughter, and General Calhoun beat it down by banging a glass ash tray repeatedly on the desk. Grover scowled and showed his puckish temperament. "Captain, is it not true that you imprisoned the agent, Earl Grover, and his assistant and held them incommunicado for more than a month?"

"That's correct, Senator."

Grover took heart and plunged on. "Do you consider this a lawful procedure, Captain?"

"No, and I never claimed that it was."

"Then your own admission is that your action was based on a presumption of guilt?"

"Certainly. I had established the guilt of the involved parties in my own mind, and it only remained a matter of time to establish it in the minds of everyone." He leaned forward and smiled. "And, Senator, that's exactly what I'm going to do at this hearing."

Grover's expression soured. "What would you say, Captain, if I told you that I could produce witnesses who would testify that they would reject you for service under their command?"

"I'd say that you were on the verge of embarrassing yourself, Senator. Let me set you straight on something: The army is still the army, and Colonel So-and-So may not want me because I'm partially disabled, and he may say so to Major What's-His-Name, and I might not be accepted, as you say. But for the colonel to get in this chair and swear he did that to a fellow officer with an unmarked record would be unthinkable. If he did do it, he would never again have the confidence of any officer serving under him." He leaned back and smiled. "So go ahead and produce your witness, Senator. Ask him that question."

Loren Grover retreated into silence, and General Calhoun looked at the others. "Any further questions, gentlemen? If not, we will consider that the captain has stated his case and is prepared to follow through with it."

"I have a question," Paul Augusta said. "Captain Early, I'm not sure any man could answer this honestly, but what were your exact motives in this matter? Genuine concern for the plight of the Indians? Or a feeling that if you succeeded on a grand scale your military future would be more secure?"

Early brushed a finger against his moustache. "Senator, I would like to say that I was motivated by a feeling of largess, but I honestly can't. Yet at the same time I realized that my tenure of service was drawing to a close and there was nothing I could do to halt it. Being passed over at the last retirement board was a matter of necessity; there was a job for me, a final job. I wanted to serve well—I've always wanted to serve well—but when I took the job, I was content to keep a tidy house and let it go at that. The visit to the reservation changed my mind. Now if you want to think that I had the welfare of the Indians in the fore of my mind, that is your privilege. If you want to think my motives political, you may do that also. I honestly don't know. Perhaps a little of each, but what the percentages are I couldn't say."

Ronald Estes said, "Captain, isn't it true that you

and Colonel Barlow have never looked upon each other with favor?"

"Yes. We were never friends. But by the same token, I never tried to get anything on Colonel Barlow. I never felt that it was necessary, for my apparent handicaps definitely limited my opportunity for promotion and therefore the incentive to get anything on him or harm his career in any way."

Grover snapped, "What do you call what you're doing now, Captain?"

Early looked steadily at him. "I am going to terminate his career, sir. Terminate it finally and completely, because he does not deserve to serve in any capacity. When I have finished presenting my evidence, no one in this room will doubt the justice of that judgment."

Loren Grover bit his lip and fell silent. General Calhoun looked around to see if anyone had any further questions, then he looked at John Early. "Captain, are you prepared to give the clerk a list of witnesses who will offer supporting testimony to your charges stated in the paper you distributed?"

"Yes, sir."

"The clerk will compile the list and have the marshal summon the witnesses for future testimony. Have the billeting officer provide suitable quarters. Proceed with the list, Captain."

It took a few minutes, but Early gave the clerk the names of those involved or having direct knowledge. When he was finished, Loren Grover caught Calhoun's eye.

"General, we've been at this an hour or more, and it's damned hot. I propose a brief recess."

Calhoun thought about it a moment, then said, "The hearing will resume at one o'clock. Captain, I want to see you in my quarters in thirty minutes."

The newsmen rushed out, trying to be first at the telegrapher's office. Early took his time, letting the pack and crush thin before leaving the building. Captain Dundee and several other officers waited at the entrance, and when he came up, Dundee took his arm. "How about a drink, John?"

"I can use that," Early said, and they stepped into the officers' lounge next door and lined up at the bar.

When they had their drinks, Dundee said, "You're going to have to watch that Senator Grover, John. He wants to hang your hide over his mantle."

A major standing down the bar said, "Captain, I heard your testimony, and frankly, until I heard it, I thought that—well, that many of the things in your paper were exaggerations. But you convinced me that you're ready to prove every damned one of them. I watched Grover's face while you testified, and I think he's suddenly convinced that you can do it, too."

"He'd better be," Early said evenly, "because I can."

Captain Dundee laughed. "I've got a brother-in-law serving with Major Cohill at the Crow Agency, and he writes me that the major is turning the reservation upside down and really cleaning house."

"Then we've accomplished something," Early said. "A man always hopes that the last whoop he makes will be a loud one." He checked his watch. "Thank you for the drink, gentlemen, but General Calhoun is not a man who appreciates tardiness."

He tapped two fingers against the beak of his kepi, smiled, and walked out. He turned toward Quarters

A. The orderly let him in; the general was in the library, smoking, looking out the window, and he turned when Early came in.

"John, I rather thought that Senator Grover would want to talk. He'll be here in fifteen minutes. So will the others."

"I don't understand, General."

"The deal, man. We're going to be offered the deal."

"Already, sir?"

General Calhoun laughed softly. "John, until you testified, the Senator wasn't really positive just how well the carbine was loaded. He knew that he was in for a clawing, but he wasn't convinced it would be all that serious. You gave excellent testimony, John; it had a ring to it, and no man in that room missed it. Grover certainly didn't. I don't believe he knew until then how much his son had lied to him, deceived him."

The orderly announced Senators Estes and Augusta; they came in, smiled, shook hands with John Early, then accepted the drink the general offered.

Estes said, "Senator Burger sends his regrets, but he has some correspondence to catch up on." He stood by the front window. "Here comes Loren now. I wonder what he said to his son."

Grover came in, gave his hat and cane to the orderly, then poured a drink for himself. He looked at Calhoun and the others, then at John Early. "Captain, the last time I spoke to you in private, I made some intemperate remarks about your honesty. Will you accept my apology for them?"

"Of course, Senator. I'm afraid neither of us knew the other very well."

"That's very kind of you," Grover said, his manner mild.

"I'd like to remind everyone that our recess is short," Calhoun said.

"Yes, I hadn't forgotten that," Grover said. "So to the point. You are ready to put my son in prison, aren't you? You're ready to go to the end of the road."

"I was ready to do that before I ever saw you, sir," Early said.

Grover sighed. "I suppose they're good witnesses, as you say. All people with sound reputations? I was sure when I heard your testimony." He put his glass down. "If you send my son to prison, all you're going to get out of it is satisfaction, Captain. It will remove him from Pine Ridge but in no way assure you that the same thing will not happen again, with another man." He lifted his hand, holding Early silent. "I'm going to be frank with you; I want to keep my son out of prison, and I want to minimize the damage such a sentence could do to my career. I don't give a damn about the Indians, or even you, Captain, but I'm willing to bargain to save my own reputation and the freedom of my son."

General Calhoun said, "What did you have in mind, Senator?"

"The committee will render a decision that will not involve criminal action," Grover said. "By that I mean that the decision can stipulate that although irregularities did occur, restitution will be made and personnel will be changed to prevent a repetition of it. The committee will also recommend that General Spencer be relieved of his command and that Captain

Early be promoted to lieutenant colonel and given the post, with full powers to regulate affairs relating to Indians within the sphere of his command."

"That's a damned bribe!" Early flared up.

Grover pointed his finger. "It's the only way you're going to get the job done, Captain, if that's what you really want to do. And if it's all been a plot to further your career—well, you've done that, too."

"We can't terminate this investigation," Augusta said. "The newspapers would tear us to pieces."

"Yes, but we can control the questions asked the witnesses and tone it down," Grover said. "Gentlemen, my alternative is both reasonable and just. I leave you now to think about it. General, when the investigation begins again in—" he looked at his watch—"eighteen minutes, I will know by the questions you ask whether or not my offer has been accepted or refused. Think about it."

He left the building then, and Calhoun poured another round of drinks. John Early said, "Sir, I refuse to—"

"Don't be hasty," Estes said quickly. "Your military training ought to point up the foolishness of that." He scratched his chin. "What are we trying to do, gentlemen? Redress wrongs or merely gather evidence to turn in an indictment to the first federal judge?"

"If it's that," Augusta said, "we really need go no further than Captain Early. I agree that our purpose is one of broader concept. General?"

"Yes," Calhoun said. "Of course, we'll be throwing General Spencer away, in a sense. A general is not relieved of his command without some repercussions."

"If we go on through with this and fight Grover," Estes said, "we are most certainly going to lose Captain Early. Grover will see to it, and you all know that he can do it." He looked intently at Calhoun. "General, of the two men, who is more likely to correct this situation? John Early or Adam Spencer?"

"That's a hell of a question!" Calhoun snapped.

"And that's no answer."

"All right, John Early," Calhoun said. "Do you want to accept Grover's offer?"

"I think it's the wisest course," Augusta said. "It will also give us a grip on the Senator and perhaps bring him under a more satisfying control."

"May I offer an opinion?" Early asked. "Just what do you think my fellow officers are going to think if I'm jumped on the promotion list after being held back all these years? I'll tell you what they'll think. They'll think I sold out for a silver oak-leaf."

"The recommendation will come from the committee," Calhoun said. "And you can't escape some speculation, John. My God, man, I'd think you'd be used to it by now." He consulted his watch. "It's time to go. We're agreed then? John?"

"I have misgivings," Early said, "but I agree. I hope I'm not sorry."

Chapter Eleven

Capt. John Early remained an additional week at Fort Laramie, and then, without fanfare or attention being aroused, orders were cut and signed by General Calhoun, relieving General Spencer of his command and appointing John Early to the post.

As soon as he assumed command, Early sent telegrams to Major Andress at the Standing Rock Agency, and Major Cohill at the Crow Agency, and to Lieutenant Colonel Jahns at the Pawnee Agency, advising them of the change. John Early was not concerned because these men ranked him; his authority was General Calhoun's authority, and these commanders understood that, even while they disliked it.

Gen. Adam Spencer's surrender of the command was a friendless affair; he plainly blamed Early for all his difficulties, and Early did nothing to change the man's mind because he didn't care what Spencer thought.

The investigation continued, with the committee calling witnesses and questioning them very carefully. Senator Grover knew that his son was guilty, but they could control the apparent degree of that guilt by the testimony they admitted into the record. Stella Parish was not called, and Lieutenant Prine was not called, and in ten days they had heard enough and retired to consider their recommendation.

Some of the newspapermen were disappointed, for they expected more color—Senators losing their tempers and witnesses shouting and pointing; there was none of that. The whole investigation took on a quiet tone, and when the committee announced that it would render a decision at ten o'clock, the room was jammed with reporters and the curious.

The committee, after due consideration of all the facts, found that irregularities did exist at the Pine Ridge Agency and that Earl Grover was responsible for them. He had mishandled supplies and poorly administrated agency affairs, although the profit motive had not been definitely established.

It was the committee's recommendation that Earl Grover be dismissed permanently from government service and made to render, in cash, the amounts deficit on agency accounts.

The implication of Col. George Barlow had not been clearly proved, yet sufficient evidence existed to recommend his immediate retirement from the service; the letter of resignation had already been received by the committee. Dan Marley, Len Kelly, and Orin Davis, involved by association, were denied future employment with the United States Government and would henceforth be liable themselves to criminal action by setting foot on government lands, posts or reservations.

The committee adjourned, and the newsmen made a race to the telegraph.

Many were critical of the committee's action and recommendation. Some were satisfied, while others thought it turned out just as they had always said i would—a little bargaining here and there, a little political give-and-take.

Calhoun invited John Early to his quarters for a farewell drink; the orderly had already packed, and Calhoun was leaving on the late train. "We won't satisfy them all with this decision, John, but it's up to you to see that we made the right one."

"Yes, sir. I'm leaving for an inspection trip in the morning."

"As soon as I get to Washington, I'll see that the recommendation is put in for your promotion. It's only a question of time, John."

"General, I'm not going to worry about it," Early said. He finished his drink, shook hands, and left. As he walked toward his own quarters, he saw Col. George Barlow step out just as he passed, and he stopped because he didn't want Barlow to think that he was avoiding him.

Barlow said, "Well, John, you really didn't do badly, did you?"

"I wanted more," Early said. "Especially with Earl Grover."

"And for me?"

"You were just a fool," Early said frankly. "But you'd gone too far, George, no matter what the reasons are."

"If you had any idea what this has done to my wife—"

"George, the world doesn't turn on your wife's pleasure. I hope you find something. Your record's clean. There's nothing on paper to stare you in the face."

"Just talk," Barlow said. "And you know what that can do to a man."

"If he lets it," Early said and walked on to his own quarters.

That evening he packed his things and made arrangements to have a saddle and a pack horse waiting for him right after morning mess. Then he bathed, shaved, and went to bed early.

Before dawn he woke and was the first at the mess; he ate quickly and went to his quarters for his things. A trooper had lashed his gear on the pack horse, and Early was suddenly eager to quit the post and get on with his duties. He knew that any delay would make his job more difficult, for it would give the commanders a chance to throw the rug over anything amiss in their commands, but he counteracted this in a small way by not announcing his arrival at any of the agencies.

As soon as he left the post, he swung southeast. In two days' riding he reached Fort Sidney and threw the officer of the day into a panic with this unexpected arrival.

Lt. Col. Howard Jahns commanded, and his responsibilities embraced the entire Pawnee reservation; he was not on the post but at agency headquarters, supervising a large beef ration.

"In the middle of the week, Lieutenant?" Early asked. "Provide me with an escort, and I'll join the colonel on the reservation." He held up a finger and wagged it. "And don't make the mistake of rushing to the telegrapher as soon as I clear the post."

A sergeant and three enlisted men appeared with saddled horses. After seeing that his pack horse was unloaded and stabled, Early remounted, and they left the post, taking an easterly direction. It was a three-hour ride to reservation headquarters, and even a mile away they could see the column of dust raised by the beef issue. To satisfy the Indians' lust to hunt, each steer was freed for a mad dash across the stable yard, with the brave pursuing it for the kill. Once the slaughter was made, the brave retired and let the women butcher.

This went on from dawn to dark, a dusty, odorous business, but it kept the Indians happy.

Col. Howard Jahns was a frail man with a gray moustache and a grave, thoughtful manner. He worked with the agent in a constant swirl of dust, checking the issue sheets as the steers were let out for their final run. And he didn't see John Early until Early was dismounting, and then Jahns hastily turned the duty over to a lieutenant and came over.

Together they walked toward headquarters, and Jahns flogged dust from his clothes with his gloves. They went inside, and although the office was oven-hot, it was quieter, and Jahn got out the bottle and glasses.

"Congratulations on your command, Captain," Jahns said. "I don't envy you in the slightest."

"Thank you," Early said, taking his drink. "Where's the agent and his civilian staff?"

"On the reservation. Doing his job. One of my officers and a squad are with him."

"To see that he does his job or to help him?"

Jahns laughed. "A little of both, I suppose. All is not as it should be, Captain, but things are improving. I can guarantee that. The beef issue is taking place now with regularity, every two weeks. There was some trouble getting the cattlemen to sell for script, but that's been solved."

"I won't tolerate one dammed bit of irregularity, Colonel," John Early said flatly. "You have a large reservation here and a grave responsibility—nevertheless we'll give the Indians a fair shake. No cheap goods, Colonel, no shorting the supplies, and no cull beef. The government funds are sufficient to furnish good quality. I mean to see that they get it."

Jahns did not take personal offense; he nodded and said, "Captain, I'm assuming that with the responsibility of your new command a rank commensurate with that responsibility is forthcoming. But with that aside, I feel as much responsibility toward my assignment as you do. These Indians are not easy to work with, Captain. They are without pride and ambition and seem almost determined not to help themselves. Teaching them anything will be difficult, if not impossible."

"We have beaten the Indian, and now we want him to act as though he had not been beaten at all," Early said. "About that there is little or nothing we can do, and I'm not sure we should do anything if we could. Our job is to see that the Indian has food and land to live on and that he doesn't freeze in the winter. If he is given employment at the agency, in addition to his small allotment, then he is to be paid for it. We're to see that he's treated honestly and fairly, keeping out independent traders and whiskey peddlers. In short, Colonel, we're going to run a clean store. And the Indians, as at Pine Ridge, may not believe it, but they appreciate it. In time—but likely not in yours and mine—the Indian may take hold again and raise himself. We can hope so, and that's all." He took a cigar from his shirt pocket and lit it. "May I use your telegraph, Colonel? I want a meeting of post commanders at Camp Sheridan on the tenth of next month." He consulted a wall calendar. "That's sixteen days from now. It's time to develop policy instead of proceeding on an individualistic basis."

As soon as he returned to Camp Sheridan, John Early had Gen. Adam Spencer's old headquarters staff moved from Fort Laramie and placed in a wing of the headquarters building. Lieutenant Deacon put a detail to work setting up a partition and turning one large room into two offices, and Early spent much of his time at a desk, writing and rewriting a step-by-step program that would put the agencies on an honest, progressive basis. Schools would have to be reactivated; they had been closed down now for nearly two years. And the church people would want to come back. They were, in Early's opinion, a blessing and a curse. A blessing because the time a man spent on his knees was never wasted, and a curse because religion was in headlong conflict with the tribal medicine man, who was still all-powerful.

He had been back a week when the mail courier arrived from Fort Robinson with newspapers and three dispatches. Robinson had a new commanding officer, a light colonel Early knew slightly. There was a dispatch from General Calhoun, offering Early his best wishes and telling him that the newspaper treatment of the hearing and Early's testimony assured him of his promotion; Grover had already offered up a resolution on the floor, and a vote was pending.

The third dispatch was from Farnam & Co. of Yankton, offering blankets, hardware, and general food supplies at rates substantially below what had been offered. Farnam & Co. also bought and sold cattle and advised John Early that an agent would call and discuss the business opportunities.

The newspapers, when Early got around to reading them, were varied in their reaction to the committee's recommendation; some felt that politics had taken precedence over justice, and the editorials were quite strong and pointed. Others felt that the committee had maintained a clear course and had done what was best for the reservation Indians, which was the whole idea behind the purge.

In the Laramie paper Early noticed a small announcement that Gen. Adam Spencer was retiring from military service and had disclosed plans for returning to the East, where he intended going into business for himself. This surprised Early, for Spencer wasn't in that much trouble. He had largely failed to carry out his duties in a thorough, aggressive manner, but he had done nothing actionable, and his career was not in danger. True, he had a cloud on him, but a lot of officers had that, and it was hardly reason for retirement.

The notice bothered John Early a little.

Ken Parish, the older boy, came to the post on a Thursday morning, and Early gave him a note to take back to his mother—an invitation for her to come to the post on Saturday and remain all day Sunday.

Camp Sheridan was a good piece south of the agency, and it would be a six-hour buggy ride for her. Early supposed that he was presuming a lot in asking her to come, but his duties prevented him from leaving, and he wanted to see her, to talk to her, to be with her for a time.

Ken Parish was sure that she'd be glad to come, and the issue hung on that boyish assurance when he left the post.

After evening mess Early invited Lt. Phil Ewing to his office, offered him a cigar and a good chair, then said, "How do you like being a post commander, Phil?"

"I have a lot less time for myself," Ewing said.

"Enjoying your paper work?"

"Hell, no, sir."

"But the heavier the duty, the more paper work you can count on, right?"

"Yes, sir," Ewing said. "The captain has a point, I feel."

Early rubbed his cheek and scratched his head under the elastic eye band. "Phil, I've been working a few days now on a system of accounting for the four agencies under my command. As it is now, each agent is completely independent, keeps his own books in his own way, and the whole thing is so loose that an agent could steal and we'd have a hard time catching him. If he says he's got eighteen barrels of cornmeal, then we have to take his word." He drew on his cigar and blew the smoke toward the low ceiling. "I'd like to set up a complete warehousing system here at Camp Sheridan. It would be necessary to build two more buildings. Supplies would be stored here and moved to the agencies as they were requisitioned. In payment for the supplies as they were delivered here, this office would draw vouchers on the individual agents' accounts."

"Who would be in charge, sir?"

"I was thinking of Lieutenant Prine, Phil. Do you think he would accept a transfer here?"

"Yes, sir, I think he'd jump at it."

"I'll prepare a wire to his commanding officer," Early said, and made a note of it on a piece of paper. "Now, having closed the loopholes in the supply system, it is necessary to minimize the opportunity for funny business once the supplies leave here. This does not imply that the other agents would sell the supplies as Grover did, but we ought to plug that hole. My only answer is random inspections of the agencies. Unannounced visits, with full reports to this office."

"Sir, we just don't have the officer force to do that."

"Why do they have to be officers?" Early asked. "Phil, if Sergeant Deeter told you something, or Rafferty, or McKeever, would you believe them?"

"Certainly. They're reliable men with long records of good service." He smiled then. "I see what you're getting at. They simply show up at an agency, spend a few days, talk to the Indians, roam around, and come back with a report."

"Correct. And no one would ever suspect their real purpose." He leaned back in his chair and studied Ewing. "Putting it bluntly, the largest mistake I can make is to trust blindly Andress, Cohill, and Jahns simply because they're officers. That was General Spencer's mistake; he wired them and asked them how things were, and they told him things were just grand, and he sat on his butt and let it go at that." Early shook his head. "I won't make that mistake. Phil, the army is changing, and officers are changing with it, for better or worse, and only time can tell that. Ten years ago a man could do his tour at some frontier post and make his promotions and know that there were still battles to be won. Now he knows there are no more battles, and other than training troops and keeping house, there's nothing for him. Even recruitment has stopped now, and it may be some time before it picks up. What does an officer do? Parades, patrols, post duty—he finds himself with time on his hands and opportunity to make money all around him, and yet he isn't able to take advantage of it. I don't rely too much on a man's ability to resist temptation. I've seen the time when it was difficult to resist it myself."

"I find that hard to believe, sir."

Early laughed softly. "Phil, a man has to be frozen in rank a number of years before he begins to feel that he's doing a lot of chopping and no chips are flying. He's like a vessel froze in ice, still working the ship, but getting nowhere. Things look good about then, Phil—a chance here to make some money by changing an order or looking the other way. But an officer just can't do that. There can be no exceptions. I'm sure George Barlow felt that he was doing the only thing possible, but it just wasn't so." He smiled and got up. "You've very carefully avoided asking me about the hearing; there's no need for that. When Senator Grover became convinced that I intended to go through with it, present one witness after another and put his son behind bars, he offered a deal. And I accepted it. He kept his son out of prison, and I assumed command over six thousand Indians. I could have refused the command, Phil, stood by and watched some incompetent bungle his way along and have been powerless to stop him. Now the responsibility is mine, and the bargain I made with my conscience was done for the good of the service." He took out Calhoun's dispatch and showed it to Lieutenant Ewing. "If you want to think of this promotion as a bribe, feel free to do so. But we will nevertheless clean up the reservations."

"Captain, you should have been a chicken colonel four years ago," Ewing said. "Congratulations may be premature, but I'm offering them just the same."

"Thank you, Phil. In a few days now we'll be having a meeting of commanding officers, two majors and a light colonel. I want to impress upon you that a first lieutenant's rank is a cut or two below theirs, but I will expect a full contribution from you. None of this sitting there with no opinions. Understood?"

"Yes, sir."

"That will be all then," Early said, "and thank you for coming."

After Ewing went out, Early sat behind his desk and worked on a program for the meeting; his planning had to be thorough because he was not certain of any of them, even Howard Jahns. If any of them were cheating the scheme, they would mask that fact because they all knew that a close look was being taken of everythng and that Early's future depended on his digging until he found it.

It was possible, Early thought, that all of them

could be sincere, dedicated men, but the possibility remained that they might not be either. Barlow had succumbed to pressure, and they were no stronger than he had been.

Who really is, Early wondered. All men break after a time, and there are levers and wedges that can be used to produce an early rupture of a man's moral fiber. A man loved too well or owed too much, and there was the crack, just waiting for a pry to be inserted. When a man had something to lose, then he became vulnerable.

Perhaps, he thought, that's been my strength, not having anything to lose, and he wondered what Stella Parish would say when she learned that he was going to be promoted to colonel in one fell swoop. And it mattered to him what she would say and think, and it worried him, because no matter how one looked at it, it didn't look right. A few men had from time to time been jumped over the heads of others, and those men were never popular. Custer hadn't been; he'd even quarreled with a President.

There were men in the service who would never understand this pending promotion, and he would not be able to justify, in their eyes, the skipping on the list. They all knew that he was a captain, frozen there long ago, and this sudden thawing was too much of a surprise. He could clean up this mess, give every Indian on reservation a college education, and still there would be men who would claim that he'd "dealed" his way into the rank by squeezing a Senator's son.

And they would be right, Early thought, for he had done that. Not intentionally, but he hadn't fought very hard, either. He supposed that he really had felt denied, deprived, cheated all these years; he didn't want to feel that way, but it was there—the desire to be recognized, to be elevated in a service where he had given so much.

Col. John Early.

Three years more and he'd hold the rank long enough to retire and draw a sizable pension, enough to make him and his wife comfortable all their lives, and perhaps leave enough for him to go into business. He was a careful man, a saving man, and he had a considerable amount put away in the Tucson bank—nearly eight thousand dollars gouged out of his poor salary and allowances.

It felt good to sit there alone, with the sun going down, and feel greedy—to be avaricious and to enjoy it. A man should allow himself a little selfishness, he thought, but it took hope to do that, and until now he had had no real hope of extending his service life. But he might be four or five years at this command, and that possibility raised new areas of speculation for him.

He was still amused to be thinking like this; it was alien to him, for he had long ago divorced himself from ambition. Now he was thinking of a wife and retirement with an impressive rank, and it was almost funny, for he was as eager as a new lieutenant wishing to distinguish himself and get a notation in a dispatch, a commentary on his record.

Suddenly he laughed out loud and slapped the top of the desk; he felt a bit foolish, and all at once he didn't give a damn any more, and that was the best feeling of all—to go loose inside and not to care about the future. Because a man's future was that moment following the one he now lived and extended no further than that. Not into tomorrow or next week, it was that moment just around the corner, so close a man could almost touch it, yet close enough for him to feel anticipation about it.

John Early knew the truth then, and it was a satisfying thing. He didn't care whether he became a colonel or not. He had life and his work and a woman he knew he could love, and what the hell else was there?

Nothing, he decided, and any man who felt otherwise was a fool.

Chapter Twelve

Lt. Murray Butler, whose whereabouts was always a question, returned to the post two hours after Stella Parish and her sons arrived. Lieutenant Kitchen, who was officer of the day, said nothing about it because dinner was being served in Early's quarters and Kitchen didn't want to disturb him with trivial matters.

After dinner Early and Stella Parish sat on his porch, and the boys went to see Sergeant McKeever. He was a favorite of theirs and had a way with boys, and all this suited John Early because he wanted to talk to Stella Parish alone.

The sun was down and darkness was falling fast, yet it was that halfway station between daylight and dark. He saw Lieutenant Butler limping painfully from the mess, walking wearily toward his quarters at the end of the row.

"Excuse me," Early said. "Mr. Butler! Oh, Mr. Butler! Over here!" Butler stopped, located the voice, then walked on over. When he came up, Early said, "You're limping, Mr. Butler. Have you hurt yourself?"

Butler craned his neck, peered through his thick glasses, then smiled and nodded. "Good evening, Captain—Mrs. Parish. Hurt myself? I had an unfortunate incident, Captain. Most unfortunate. One I don't understand myself."

"Tell me about it," Early urged.

"Very well, if you like mystery," Butler said. "I was in Yankton some days ago—I forget how many exactly. I had ordered some supplies and thought I might as well ride in and meet the train. They were rather delicate, and I didn't want them broken by some clumsy teamster. You know how they are, Captain. A very careless lot." He paused. "What was I saying?"

"The mystery."

"Oh, yes. Well, while in Yankton, I accidentally bumped into a man on the street. I was knocked down, and I lost my glasses, and while I was groping for them, the man cursed me. Of course, I must be mistaken, but it seemed to be the same officer who was rude to me for making smoke on the parade ground. He was with someone else, and they hurried on and were turning into a building when I found my glasses, wiped them, and put them on. Isn't that odd, Captain?"

Early was leaning forward in his chair, his attention sharp. "Go on, Mr. Butler. Your story is very interesting. Would you recognize the building if you saw it again?"

"Yes. I saw the sign. Farnum & Co."

"Ah," Early said with a long sigh. "Go on."

Butler shook his head. "It's very confusing to me, Captain. I got my supplies and was riding back when this shot rang out and my horse fell, rolling on my leg. Fortunately the ground was a bit damp and soft or I'd surely have broken it." He peered curiously at John Early. "Why would anyone want to kill my horse, Captain? It was a long walk back, and I now have a crop of blisters."

"Mr. Butler, I want you to put yourself in Dr. Mulvahill's care and rest for a few days. Will you do that for me?"

"Yes, I believe I will. Good night, Captain—Mrs. Parish."

After he'd walked away, Early said softly, "My, that's bold. Very bold."

"What is, John?"

"George Barlow," he said. "Don't you see what it is? George Barlow has gone into business for himself in Yankton. I had a communication from Farnum & Co. offering a very attractive rate on supplies and hardware." He sat back, deep in thought. "George wouldn't be in this alone. No, he doesn't have that kind of nerve. And, of course, there's the shot that was fired at Butler—they meant to kill him. Marley probably fired that, and where there's Marley, there's Earl Grover."

Stella said, "John, would they be so greedy for money that they'd risk—"

He laughed and shook his head. "No, they're after me. I don't understand how, but they're going to make sure they sell to the agency and implicate me so that I'll go out the way George Barlow and Grover did." He lit a cigar and smoked a moment. "Stella, you know without my telling you that I invited you here to propose. You did know that, didn't you?"

"Well, I'd rather hoped that was the reason," she admitted.

"The boys could stay here, if you liked, and we could drive to Yankton and get married. I could also look into this matter and not have it pop up later and interfere with our settling down."

She smiled in a small, half-hidden way. "John, you're selling me a bill of goods."

"I'm trying to tell you that I love you, and I'm doing a bad job of it, Stella."

She shook her head. "No, you did fine. When did you want to leave?"

"In the morning if it suits you."

"Yes, but I'm going to send the boys home. We'll be gone a week, and there are chores to be done." Then she leaned over and kissed him. "Now I'll have to worry about what to wear."

"We'll buy everything new in Yankton," he said, laughing. "We'll take an ambulance to Valentine and catch the stage there. We'll have a good life, Stella. I know we will."

"John, I was almost sure of that the first time I ever met you." She got up and stood by his chair a moment, then bent and kissed him. "Good night."

They had a three-hour wait for the stage at Valentine, and John Early gave Stella forty dollars because she had found a dressmaker on a side street and there was a dress in there she just knew would fit her. It pleased him to give her money; he had never given a woman money before, and while she fussed in there, he went to the main street and the general store and bought a brown suit with two pairs of pants for twelve dollars. A derby and a pair of shoes made a new man of him, and he walked back toward the dress shop, the shoes squeaking at each step.

When they got on the stage, Stella had a hatbox and a small valise, and Early was carrying a satchel; he put all these things in the boot and took the seat beside her.

The stage took eighteen hours for the run from Valentine to Yankton because the terrain was rough and there was a high mountain pass to pull up and they stopped at three way stations in the climb, for the teams had to be changed.

Yankton, after going through the population boom of the mining days, had finally stabilized, and other, less glamorous, but steadier industries had taken over to support the town. There were still some mining and smelting going on, but timber was a big thing, and cattle and some sheep helped steady the economy, and there were farmers with their plowed fields and crops and families. All these things had an influence on the community.

As soon as they got off the stage, Early and Stella went to the hotel; he deposited his bags with the clerk and registered as man and wife. As he spun the register around, he said, "Can you recommend a minister?"

The clerk looked up. "I beg your pardon."

"A minister. A man of the cloth. A religious individual who performs the marriage ceremony."

"You two want to get married," the clerk said.

John Early smiled. "You are an unusually bright lad. Yes, you have grasped the whole thing in one fell swoop."

"There's a Baptist minister who lives on Poke Street." He pointed. "Two blocks over. You can see the steeple from the corner. Parsonage is to the right."

"Thank you," Early said. He took Stella Parish by the arm. "Shall we?"

"I would hate to come this far and be disappointed."

They left by the side door and walked halfway down the street before Early came to a halt. "The ring!" he said. "I forgot to buy a ring!" He bowed. "My dear, could I induce you to do an about-face, return to the main street and the general store where we can select a ring?"

"We can get married without a ring," she said.

"Oh, I know, but years later we may regret it. Please, Stella?"

She smiled and nodded, and they retraced their steps to the main street. Early paused to look up and down, searching for the largest store, he found one, and they turned left and went down half a block.

Cassidy's boasted a complete line of merchandise, including the new Sears & Roebuck line of buggies and farm implements. After a moment of wandering about, Early and Stella Parish stopped before a jewelry showcase. Instantly Early saw what he wanted—a heavy band of gold with forget-me-nots delicately carved into the circumference.

The clerk came over, and Early pointed. "How much for that ring?"

It was taken from the case. "Solid gold, mister. Ninety dollars."

"You have just sold it," Early said and paid the clerk, who gave it to Cassidy to ring up. Stella was tugging at Early's sleeve and frowning. He said, "What's the matter?"

"Are you insane, John?" She kept her voice to a

whisper. "Ninety dollars for a ring? Why, for a couple years there I didn't show that much profit!"

"And there were some years when I thought I didn't make that much," he said, "but this is something I want you to have. I don't think I can accurately put a price on it." He stopped talking as the clerk came back, all smiles.

"May I offer congratulations?" the clerk said. "Lucky man, lovely woman." He glanced away as someone came in, and Early followed his glance because it was a natural thing to do.

Then he turned full face and looked at Earl Grover and Dan Marley, and they looked at him, recognized him, and then Grover bolted out the door. Marley put his hand under his coat and kept it there and slowly backed toward the door, feeling for it with his free hand. He stepped through, still backing, then hurried across the street and stood on the other side, facing the store, his hand still beneath his coat.

The clerk was uneasy now. "Do you know Mr. Patterson and Mr. Corday, sir?"

"The one who dashed out is Earl Grover. The one across the street is Dan Marley," Early said. He looked steadily at the clerk. "Where is their partner?"

"Office down the street," the clerk said. "You'll find them both there, I imagine."

"Both?"

He nodded. "Mr. Barlow and Mr. Spencer, sir."

Early could see out the front window. Dan Marley stopped a man who was passing, talked to him a moment, then the man crossed over and came into the store. He looked around, saw Early, then said, "He wants you to step outside, friend. I guess you know what for."

"Why don't you go on down the street and tell the sheriff?" Early said.

"None of my business," the man said and walked out.

Early stepped over to a showcase with a curved glass front and selected a long barreled pistol that had seen considerable use. The clerk, who followed him along, lifted it out, and Early cocked it, checking the action. Stella Parish started to say something, but he shook his head. "Look out the door, Stella. There's a man who feels he just can't pass up this chance." He glanced at the clerk. "How much for this pistol and some shells?"

Cassidy, who was farther down the counter, said, "Why don't you just take the loan of it? Get him a box of shells, Herbie." He left the customer he had been waiting on and stepped down toward John Early. "That man's a bruiser; he's already backed two men down in squabbles over nothing."

"I'm acquainted with Mr. Marley's personality," Early said. "Stella, wait for me here." Again she started to say something and again he shook his head. He opened the loading gate and half-cocked the pistol, filling the chamber and not leaving a dead one beneath the hammer. He dropped a dozen cartridges in his coat pocket, then put the pistol in his belt.

Cassidy said, "Herbie, go out the back way and see if you can find the sheriff."

The clerk needed no additional urging; he flung his apron down and ran out. John Early stepped to the front door, went to the edge of the walk and stopped there. Marley straightened; he kept his hand under his coat, and he watched Early with a fixed stare.

"I kind of thought I'd see you," Marley said. "On account of that damned old fool of a lieutenant, huh?" He laughed. "How did you find out?"

"He told me," Early said and watched Marley show surprise. "You got his horse. Butler walked in. Got a lot of blisters on his feet."

"I'll be damned," Marley said frankly. "I saw him go down, but it was a long way from the rimrock to the trail, so I just figured—" He stopped and laughed. "But I figured wrong, didn't I?"

"It's not the first time," Early pointed out. "And if you pull that gun, it'll just be another mistake. It's not going to be worth it to you, Dan." He turned his head and looked up and down the street; there were a dozen gaps between the buildings where Earl Grover could be hiding with a rifle. And that would be what Grover would do, because he was a man who liked every advantage.

Early said, "I hear you have a little business started up, Dan. Of course you're just a hired man, and that's all you'll ever be. Where's little Earl?"

"He's around."

"Dan, don't count on him. All he ever gave you was money. Haven't you learned that?"

"Money's enough," Marley said. "But you've gone and spoiled it, coming here." He stood there for a moment, completely still, then he yelled, "Shoot, Earl!" and drew his own gun.

John Early launched himself sideways, and from

the roof across the street a rifle boomed, and the bullet smashed through the front glass of Cassidy's store. Early struck the walk with his shoulder and had his gun out even as he rolled. Dan Marley shot twice, fanning the hammer, and the bullets scattered, one puckering dust in the street and another hitting the porch post eight feet from where Early lay.

He sighed and fired, and Dan Marley stumbled backward one step before dropping his gun and clapping both hands to his chest. He staggered like a man who has been drinking steadily and just can't get totally drunk; then his knees turned to yarn and he fell.

Early wasn't motionless; he had skinned off the walk and was now crouched down behind the heavy plank watering trough, safe from Earl Grover's rifle. He waited a moment while silence lay heavily over the street; at the first shot all traffic had stopped and pedestrians had taken cover inside the buildings.

Early gathered himself, judged the distance to the other side, then jumped up and began running, driving himself to this one effort and ignoring the pain in his bad leg. Earl Grover realized too late what was happening and flung one more shot down. It narrowly missed Early and whined away, and then it was not possible to shoot again, for Early was under the porch overhang on the other side and looking for a place to get into the alley.

He found a gap between the buildings and edged himself along it, trying not to stumble over the litter there, and finally he came out in back and saw stairs leading up.

There was a sound on the roof—a man sliding

down. Then Earl Grover let his feet dangle over the edge, and dropped to the upper porch landing, lighting on his hands and knees. He looked around and down and saw John Early standing there. For an instant he could not seem to move, then he swore and swung his rifle around.

Early tilted the muzzle of his pistol and shot and watched the rifle fall down the stairs. Earl Grover followed it, as though he could not bear to lose it. He broke through the handrail near the bottom and landed on some wooden boxes, splintering them with his weight.

Then the sheriff ran down the alley with a crowd behind him; he looked at Grover, then took Early's gun and said, "I guess you'll be willing to explain this to me, won't you?"

Chapter Thirteen

The Sheriff was a sensible man who knew the value of witnesses, and it took all of fourteen minutes to clear up the shooting. This was done in Cassidy's store, where it had all started, and John Early found that a glass of Cassidy's whiskey went a long way toward steadying him down, for he had the annoying habit of getting a case of the jitters after these tight moments in his life.

A crowd formed in the street and in the alley, but two of the sheriff's deputies kept them under control. When the sheriff was satisfied, John Early said, "The affair is not quite finished, I'm sorry to say." He laid the pistol on Cassiday's counter, taking care not to set it down too hard on the glass.

Stella Parish said, "John, leave the rest of it alone now."

"I can't," he said. "But there won't be any more trouble. George and the general both value their own skins too much to risk anything." He patted her cheek. "You're going to make a fine wife, Stella. You know how to wait for a man."

"I don't know how at all," she said. "I just know how to keep from bawling in public."

The sheriff said, "I think I'll go along with you, Captain."

"That won't be necessary," Early said, "but thanks

just the same." He stepped out of the store and cut across the street and walked a block down, casting his glance up at the signs and when he found Farnam & Co. he stopped, peered in the window, then quickly stepped to the door and opened it.

Adam Spencer was sitting at the desk, his hands clasped in front of him, his teeth gently nibbling at the inside of his lower lip. George Barlow walked back and forth. They both looked up together, Spencer raising his head and Barlow half turning.

John Early said, "You were expecting someone else, I know. Earl is dead. In the alley. He just was never lucky at anything, I guess." He stepped deeper into the room and stopped with his thighs resting against the edge of Spencer's desk. "General, I just don't know what to say to you. You disappoint me. Revenge? Really, that's for the little man, the man you've always despised." He looked at George Barlow. "You just never did learn when you were well off, did you?"

There was a noise in back, a door opening and closing, and Spencer started to reach for a desk drawer. Early shoved against the desk, cramping into him, crowding him.

"Don't do that, General. Leave the gun where it is."

Then the sheriff opened the inner door and stood there; he had his pistol in hand, and when he saw there was no need for it, he holstered it and came up to Barlow and patted him carefully and found no gun.

John Early went around, opened the desk drawer, and took out a small .32 pocket pistol. The sheriff said, "What's the charges here, Captain?"

"I think stolen government property," Early said,

his expression moody. "Yes, I'm sure of it. Only I was supposed to buy it back, a blind pig in a poke, then when I discovered it, a U.S. marshal would conveniently call, and I wouldn't have a leg to stand on." He glanced at Adam Spencer. "Another hearing, General? Was Senator Grover all primed to swoop down and rush me out of the army and into prison?" He looked from one to the other then laughed. "Do you know what happened? What really happened? That absentminded Lieutenant Butler bumped into George on the street and lost his glasses. But he thought he recognized you, George. He told me you seemed to be the same officer who was rude to him because he made smoke on the parade ground. Isn't that a laugh, George? You and your damned grass!"

Adam Spencer said, "Butler's alive?"

"Oh, sure. Marley missed Butler and killed the horse and then was too lazy to climb down to the trail for a good look." He kept letting his smile build. "Gentlemen, that was genuinely stupid, trusting Marley. He just never could do anything right."

"He told me Butler was dead," Barlow said softly. "The man fell like a stone and didn't move for five minutes."

"Stunned by the unexpected fall," Early told him. "Bad mistake, George." He stepped back and motioned for the sheriff to take them into custody.

"Wait a minute now," Spencer said, holding up a hand. "Look, now, you made one deal. How about listening to another?"

"Only one to a customer," Early said. "I made one with the Senator and I meant to keep it. Too bad he didn't. Now his son is dead, and I think he'll be resigning. Neither of you will go to prison and not take him with you. It just isn't in your generous souls."

The sheriff said, "I've got me a couple of real important customers here, huh, Captain?"

"Bigger than any stage bandit you ever saw," Early said. "I want all the goods in the warehouse impounded and placed in the custody of U.S. marshals. If you don't, I'll telegraph General Calhoun and have the army moved in. You wouldn't want that to happen to your town, because it would look as if you didn't handle it right."

"I'll handle it right," the sheriff said and motioned for them to get outside.

Early closed the front door and went in back where boxes and bales and barrels were stacked to the ceiling. Much of the goods he recognized as having come from the Pine Ridge Agency. A lot of it, although similar, undoubtedly came from the other agencies, and he supposed that it had been quietly carted out of sutlers' warehouses either during the hearing or immediately afterward. There was other merchandise that had not been stolen, and Early supposed that this was what would have been offered him, and from the quality of it, he surely would have bought.

But the delivered goods would have been stolen property, and he could see how it would have looked, as though he had trumped up the whole thing and done it all to make a small fortune.

He locked the back door and went out front until the sheriff came back with a chain and lock. "Wired the U.S. marshal in Sioux City," the sheriff said. "Everything's under control, Captain."

"Thank you, sheriff. I'm sure you'll handle it fine." He smiled and went back to Cassidy's store, using the rear entrance because a large crowd cluttered the porch in front and Early was in no mood to cope with them or be polite.

There was a sourness in his stomach, because he knew what the newspapers would do in the coming months. A colonel and a general on trial would make headlines and smear every sincere officer serving his country, and yet there was nothing that could be done about it, for in sharing the honor of service they also shared the infrequent stains left by foolish men.

It would be felt politically when it came time to argue the budget, and General Calhoun would find his problems more difficult. Senator Grover had friends, perhaps the same kind of men he was, differing only in that they hadn't been caught. They would fight Calhoun in committee and Calhoun would defend the service, and it wouldn't be pleasant.

We'll have to give him something to balance the scale John Early thought. A good job on the reservations, perhaps, it was something to work for, doing something that no one really believed could be done. It would take a lot of detailed attention, a lot of hours, and careful adherence to the duty they all had sworn to uphold.

But he would do it, he knew he could do it, for others would feel the same shame he felt and work harder to wipe it out before the stain soaked in and permanently discolored. They had risen above the disgrace of Chivington and others, and they would rise above Barlow and Spencer.

Stella Parish was waiting in Cassidy's office; it was quieter there, more private, and she could pace a bit and bite her nails. Early peeked around the corner and winked, and she suddenly threw her arms around him and cried a little.

He said, "I'm a man with a one-track mind who likes to do what he sets out to do." He fished the ring out of his pocket and held it up, smiling. "Without running or making a fuss, what do you say we look for that church steeple and the parsonage alongside it and have the minister say those very important words so we can see whether this ring fits or not?"

She smiled and asked, "Are you sure there's nothing else you have to do? You can spare the time?"

"I am going to make the time. How's that sound?"

Her glance was steady, she was reading him carefully. "Like a man who's going to tell me that we ought to be starting back tomorrow." She poked him in the chest with her finger. "Do you want to hear how it's really going to be?"

John Early shook his head. "Surprise me later." Then he put his arm around her, and they went out the back way, down to the end of the alley where they had a clear look down the street.

And there was the church steeple, towering over the rest of the houses, plain enough for any man to see.

Wade Everett, a pseudonym for Will Cook, is the author of numerous outstanding Western novels as well as historical frontier fiction. He was born in Richmond, Indiana, but was raised by an aunt and uncle in Cambridge, Illinois. He joined the U.S. cavalry at the age of sixteen but was disillusioned because horses were being eliminated through mechanization. He transferred to the U.S. Army Air Force in which he served in the South Pacific during the Second World War. Cook turned to writing in 1951 and contributed a number of outstanding short stories to *Dime Western* and other pulp magazines as well as fiction for major smooth-paper magazines such as *The Saturday Evening Post*. It was in the *Post* that his best-known novel, *Comanche Captives*, was serialized. It was later filmed as *Two Rode Together* (Columbia, 1961) directed by John Ford and starring James Stewart and Richard Widmark. It has now been restored, as was the author's intention, with *The Peacemakers* set in 1870 as the first part and *Comanche Captives* set in 1874 as the second part of a major historical novel titled *Two Rode Together*. Sometimes in his short stories Cook would introduce characters that would later be featured in novels, such as Charlie Boomhauer who first appeared in *Lawmen Die Sudden* in *Big-Book Western* in 1953 and is later to be found in *Badman's Holiday* (1958) and *The Wind River Kid* (1958). Along with his steady productivity, Cook maintained an enviable quality. His novels range widely in time and place, from the Illinois frontier of 1811 to southwest Texas in 1905, but each is peopled with credible and interesting characters whose interactions form the backbone of the narrative. Most of his novels deal with more or less traditional Western themes—range wars, reformed outlaws, cattle rustling, Indian fighting—but there are also romantic novels such as *Sabrina Kane* (1956) and exercises in historical realism such as *Elizabeth, by Name* (1958). Indeed, his fiction is known for its strong heroines. Another common feature is Cook's compassion for his characters who must be able to survive in a wild and violent land. His protagonists make mistakes, hurt people they care for, and sometimes succumb to ignoble impulses, but this all provides an added dimension to the artistry of his work.